MARTIN FINE BOOK 2

RUMBLE IN THE JUNGLE

by John Kweli

ISBN 978-1-960378-42-2   (paperback)
ISBN 978-1-960378-43-9   (ePub)

1st Edition

Book design by Anna Hall

RUMBLE IN THE JUNGLE

*To Val, who rescued this
from the trash heap.*

CHAPTER

1

THE DIAMONDS GLINTED in the sun as they fell toward the black sand, and his eyes retraced their path, following it back to their source. The dream was always the same—as was the end. The rain of diamonds always ended in a gusher of blood. He shuddered and awoke in the twisted, sweat-drenched sheets. He knew the image would never leave him. If only it weren't so God-awfully raw.

His head was pounding. Tequila offered temporary respite at a high price. Food for thought at some point, but not now.

The door buzzer seeped into his hazy consciousness.

Seven a.m. Who the . . . ?

"Yes?"

"I hope you look better than you sound, old boy."

It couldn't be, but it was: Major Ian Smythe-Jones. The major's old Etonian Colonel Blimp sounded as perfectly phony as it had always had. Martin hadn't thought about the major much since that terrible day at the beach on Lamu. Truth be told, he hadn't wanted to.

He wondered what the major knew about the tragic end to his adventure. Knowing him, probably every bit.

"I should be asking how you found me, but that would be a stupid question."

1

"Quite right too. You weren't trying too hard to hide."

"Like I gave a shit. Come on up, you old bastard. I'm actually dying to see you."

The funny thing was he *was*.

A moment later, the major stood in Martin's doorway. He looked exactly the same. The same shock of white hair. Those same piercing blue eyes that always twinkled with some secret humor.

They embraced. It was a real hug, most un-major like.

God, it was good to see him. Memories flooded back, and Martin teared up, hating himself for it.

"I heard about Mapende," the major said. "That was rum, my boy, seriously shitty. I don't blame you for going doggo for a bit. I can tell you some good news. It won't wipe the slate for what Russell did, but it's a start with more to come. I arranged a little diversion, and Russell didn't get the stones to the people he wanted to. Least I could do after the drama you'd been through."

"Thanks." It was hollow but the best he could manage under the circumstances. "How about a serious cuppa?"

"Good for starters." The major's gaze moved from the mattress on the living room floor to the empty tequila bottles littering the kitchen counter. "I must say, you're living pretty spartan these days. Looks like my timing might be fortuitous. You must be wondering why I've pitched up."

Martin couldn't help but feel a tinge of embarrassment for the dismal state of his studio apartment as he put a kettle on the stove. "That thought was beginning to penetrate the Tequila fumes."

"Quite. Well, on to the point then. You may remember that I was—or better, *am*—no more of an admirer of Russell than you were."

"I seem to recollect."

"How'd you like to shit in his nasty little Langley bed?"

"Major, bit of a colonial turn of phrase coming from you, and it deserves same in reply. A hundred fucking percent. All ears."

"So . . . lots has happened in the last eighteen months."

"Kind of lost track myself."

"Lost yourself in the bottle, more likely."

"Fair point, Major. So cutting to the chase . . ."

"I'm assuming that the school this isn't serious—at least not so serious that you wouldn't junk it if a better opportunity came along."

Martin shrugged. "True enough. I've been grasping at straws. Not even sure I'm going to finish my dissertation."

The major didn't look surprised. He arched an eyebrow at a pile of dirty laundry a few feet from the mattress. "Without being cruel, I don't see any evidence around here that you've any intention of doing same. So perhaps I can tempt you with an alternate plan. Our friend Russell has been naughty and playing out of school."

The tea kettle whistled, and Martin, after finding a clean mug in the all-but-bare kitchen cupboard, poured the Major a cup of black tea, making sure to add a teaspoon of sugar and, after sniffing the carton to confirm the milk hadn't gone sour, the closest thing he had to cream. "You've got my attention. Do tell."

"What do you know about Mobutu's other goodies, besides the ones you just played with?"

"I don't know. Gold, copper—"

"No, dear boy, nothing so boring and mundane. Cobalt, Uranium—all the really bloody useful stuff."

"Well, I know they're there."

The major shrugged in mock exasperation. "Yes old boy, but importantly, who wants the stuff?"

"No points, I guess, for saying us and the Russians."

"The proper answer is "Who else?""

"Hmm . . . That could cover quite a bit of territory, but realistically, not many countries."

"Really, come on, Martin. You can do better than that. Try Libya, Syria, South Africa, Pakistan, China, and North Korea for starters."

"All of those with the possible exception of South Africa are not places I'd think our sleazy buddy would be inclined to play."

"Read between the lines, Martin, like I taught you."

"Okay, so you already dropped a huge hint. Out of school. Hmm . . . I'd have to guess Syria or Libya. Thinking a bit more, I'd guess Libya. They've got the cash."

"That's my boy! Always follow the money—true in every aspect of life."

"Seriously, Russell gone rogue? Libya? Hard to figure. He's a complete asshole, but I figured a patriotic one."

"Well, normally unreliable sources have whispered in my ear that he and a fellow compatriot are seriously considering an offer from our friend Ghaddafi."

"You don't have unreliable sources, at least that you mention."

"Secret to my success, old boy. So does that peak your interest?"

"Depends."

The major sipped his tea and looked pleased. "Not bad for a colonial. Let's face it, Martin: you aren't exactly doing much now. Farting about and pretending to go to school isn't much for a man of your diverse talents."

Trust the major not only to know what was going on but call him on it.

"Like killing people and getting them killed."

"Do you want a handkerchief?"

"Fuck you. Not nice, but effective."

"You have had too much time to think, friend. You play with the big boys, you must be prepared to take the consequences. I know you loved Mapende, but she knew the risks. So did you. You signed up for the exercise. Don't forget it." The major didn't have to say the words that were probably on his mind: *Nor the fact that I bailed out your miserable ass.*

"I guess I never thanked you, did ?"

"You had other things on your mind."

"True enough, but I owe you."

The major reached into his breast pocket and tossed a fat envelope on the table.

Martin looked inside: a plane ticket, passport, and cash.

"Time to start paying. I need you, and you could use being needed. Plus, this is your chance to play silly buggers with Russell. I surmised that you would find that opportunity hard to pass up."

Martin glanced at the passport. US. Different name, of course. That told him all he needed to know. "Trent Baker, huh? So this is off the books as far as your employers are concerned."

"Not your concern, friend. But I can tell you that you had better be off the books. There are still some serious folks who are quite pissed at you."

"I figured. How come they didn't give me more shit when I came home?"

"I got a little creative and spun a little tale to the effect that you could be of use to the Langley mob in the future. They do like to butter their bread on all sides with respect to guerilla movements. As you know, the scenery can change fast in Africa. Besides, from their point of view, everything ended well enough. Still, I don't think that they'll want you underfoot so soon, especially if what I think is happening is really going down."

"Yeah right." Martin glanced at the ticket. "Kinshasa. Always wanted to go there."

"Strictly the kickoff, old man. If things go according to plan, we may be in Niger and points south and west for a spell too."

"Okay, Major, I do owe you, but why me? Be as honest as you're capable of being."

"Why, Martin, I'm shocked that you think I could be devious." The major was positively beaming—always a bad sign. "Because I need a reliable off-the-books backup. Someone that they won't expect. You fit that bill, particularly if you don't clean up too much."

"Major, I'm not a professional spook."

"Might as well be, after the Uganda job. Anyone who took care of as nasty a piece of work as Bagaza and gave the Langley lot and the rest of Amin's mob the slip is good enough for me."

"You helped."

"Yes, but I only did the planning. You did the work."

"And look what it got me."

The major was way too smart to answer that. He sat quietly and watched Martin process. He'd groomed the battlefield perfectly, and as much as Martin hated to admit it, he knew his man.

"You're such a bastard. How'd you know that I'd have a bad case of the fuck-its?"

"Been there, old man."

Martin had no problem believing that. "When are we leaving?"

"You're leaving day after tomorrow. I want a basic recce. Spot me the players we need to know. Shouldn't be difficult for a man of your talents and experience."

"Well, it's a little different landscape than Kampala. Might take me a while."

"Quite right there. Mobutu makes Amin look like what he is: a psychotic street thug. Not that he can't or won't play just as rough, but he's taken corruption to a whole different level. I'm convinced that before he's done, he'll go down as the greatest crook in international history."

"Speaking French will help. What do you want me to do when I identify the players?"

"Sit tight. I won't be more than a fortnight behind. I booked you into the Intercontinental. Mind you, it wasn't easy or cheap. I suppose you've heard about the big fight."

Ali vs. Foreman, Martin thought. *The Rumble in the Jungle.* "Just a little. Are you kidding? That's a ways off, isn't it?"

"Just three weeks, so I had to pull a few strings."

"More like pull on a rope of hundreds. Won't things be a little busy?"

"Perfectly for our purposes. What could be better cover than the fight of the century co-promoted by two of the biggest bandits in history: Don King and Mobutu Sese Seko. It'll be a chaotic mob scene. Who's going to pay any attention to the odd mzungu floating around? Remember your Tzun Tzu."

"The cockroach in the tortoise's armpit. I love it. So what's the deal?"

"Been waiting to get to that. So it seems your man Russell and a fellow piece of scum Watkins have put out feelers to the Libyans about selling some Uranium. You may not know this, but Ghaddafi has been in the market for some for a while."

"No, I didn't, but it figures. I assume that the expertise to really produce anything would come from Russia."

"Not so obvious as you would think. There's also a rogue nuclear engineer in Pakistan we're keeping an eye on. Clearly, the best way to avoid the whole issue is to keep them from getting anything to play with." The major finished his tea. "Time for you to clean up. We're off to lunch."

Martin headed for the shower. He knew better than to ask anything except, "Dress?"

"Formal, old boy. This chap is expensive."

CHAPTER

2

EXPENSIVE WAS RIGHT. Martin chafed at the tie and suit. It had been a long time—but not long enough.

"Don't look so miserable, old boy. You actually look almost respectable, but we both know better. *Le voici.* Here comes our chap. Etienne Tshishkedi."

Tshishkedi's tailoring screamed money, right down to the diamond cufflinks. The major performed the introductions in French, knowing full well Martin was also fluent, and carefully omitting any reference that would reveal what he did. "*Plus, ca change.*"

Obviously, the major was intent on Tshishkedi earning his lunch. That would take some doing. The Four Seasons oozed quiet, impeccable affluence. Martin was sure only the Major's menu would list the prices. He hadn't seen him in action for a while. A master at work. Subtle but insistent.

"So, Mobutu is as secure as he looks?"

"*Certainement*, and the more secure he is, the greedier he becomes."

"Greedy enough to back-door his current patron?

"I am not sure I understand you." Tshishkedi's face was a perfect portrait of bemusement. Two masters at work. This was only going to get better.

"Ah, *je comprends*. A few extra diamonds, *peut t'etre*. These things always happen, even in the best of families, so to speak"

"Quite, but that was not exactly what I had in mind." The major's bland expression betrayed nothing.

"*Eh bien*. What are you sniffing around about, Major?"

"Something far more valuable but less easily transported and disposed of."

"Such as?"

"Heavy metals."

Tshishkedi raised an eyebrow. "That would be most upsetting. My employer would certainly like to know of any developments on that front. What exactly have you heard?"

"Whispers, *mon ami*. That things might be getting ready to go out the back door."

Tshishkedi was awake now, sitting bolt upright, chin on cupped hands, staring directly at the major's face. "But *les Amis*, guard it very carefully. They always see reds under the bed." He chuckled. "The only people more unsubtle than the Amis are the Russians."

"Perhaps, old man, but maybe they're guarding from the wrong people."

"*Oui, c'est possible.*"

"Clearly further enquiries should be undertaken. Equally clearly, they must be completely discreet. No waves. Not even a ripple. Hard to do if you use any of the known actors."

Conversation paused while a plump waiter skillfully prepared the Caesar salad to go with their risottos.

Tshishkedi waited until they were once again alone to respond to the major. "*Vraiment*, truly agree, which I suppose is why this gentleman is here"

"Perhaps. Do you remember the business with a certain Bertain Aka, Amin, and diamonds from Shaba a while back?"

"Of course, there were many ripples from that affair. Many

upset parties." Tshishkedi turned and studied Martin carefully, as if he was committing Martin's face to memory, which of course he was.

Martin forced himself to stay relaxed and held Tshishkedi's glance just long enough to signal that he wasn't hiding anything but not long enough to issue a challenge. It was all coming back. He knew the major was watching him. First test for this semester. He ate a few bites of risotto and waited for Tshishkedi to continue.

"I seem to recall there was a young Ami involved, as well as much untidiness with Shaba and the Ananya. Did I not hear that the mzungu caused many problems and embarrassment for the Amis and Amin?"

The major smiled. "Well, I suppose that where you stand on that now depends on where you were sitting then."

"I seem to also recall that the Amis thought they had everything arranged to their satisfaction when party's unknown snatched the prize right from under their noses. The story reminded me of another clever gentleman that I have had dealings with over the years."

"No need to get personal," the major said.

Martin could have sworn the major was preening. He wasn't above it when he thought he could get away with it.

The major waited until they were served with brandy and cigars to cut to the chase.

How very British, Martin thought.

"So, my friend, you're obviously wondering why I'm standing you to this frightfully expensive lunch."

"You British always get to things the most indirect way possible. We must learn to be patient with you, is it not so?"

"You are a perceptive man, Monsieur Tshishkedi. There are parties who would like to make discreet enquiries into these rumors."

"And . . . ?"

"For the time being, they wish those to be very, very discreet, without any hint of official involvement."

"Am I to take that literally?"

"For now, yes."

That was news to Martin, but now it all fit. The major was working off the reservation, hence Martin's involvement. He glanced around, paying more attention to the surrounding tables. It looked like the normal expense-account lunch crowd, but he was suddenly more alert than he had been in months. He felt alive again, like he was coming out of a deep trance.

"*D'accord.* I understand. What is your plan?"

"You're looking at him."

"An unofficial emissary?"

"Completely."

"You trust him."

It was awkward—to say the least, Martin thought—to sit there silently while the two men discussed him as if he were a file.

"He's perfect. No one will suspect anything. Just another mzungu in town for the fight. His passport's new. Not much chance of anyone knowing different."

"Assuming he is who I suspect he is, that's all probably true, but it will take lots of time for him to position himself."

"Not if you help him. Your employer would be most grateful if he turns up anything."

"Bien sur. He, of course, knows you well also, so he will take my report seriously. When do you propose he arrive?"

"Day after tomorrow. The whispers were very unspecific as to timing. We can't take a chance if there's even a scintilla of truth to them. Could be bloody awkward for both of us. That's assuming that you can fix the visa." The Major swirled the last of his cognac, inhaled the aroma, and swallowed it. "Bloody good that was. The cigar was decent too."

"Mon ami. The least of our worries."

"No argument from me if any of this is true. If this remotely resembles what I think it could be—a rogue operation—this could be a devilishly ticklish situation. While we're at it, I think I should come totally clean with you. Martin potentially has a very personal interest in the proceedings. That's all you need to know for now."

"Okay, Martin, please come to the consulate tomorrow and go to the normal visa office. Everything will be fixed, but do not mention my name. Give me your phone number now. I will devote some thought to the situation and set up a meeting with you later tomorrow at a discreet location." Tshishkedi turned to the major. "Why is it, Major, that we always meet under difficult circumstances?"

"Because we're so grossly overpaid."

CHAPTER

3

MARTIN DULY PRESENTED himself at the Zairean consulate at ten o'clock the next morning. Mobutu wasn't skimping on accommodations. The offices were housed in a brownstone a few blocks away from the UN. Martin was glad he wasn't paying the rent.

As expected, Tshishkedi had fixed everything. Martin smiled to himself as he paid the $500 "expedite" fee. There were some things even the most powerful folks couldn't circumvent.

The expression clerk handed him an envelope, which Martin opened once he'd gotten a few blocks away and ascertained that he wasn't being tailed.

There was an expensive—but anonymous as to any useful information—Zaire government card with an address, apartment number, and time. "Eh bien," Martin thought, "back in it again." It actually felt good. Adrenalin was more potent than anything else he could put in his mouth or up his nose. The fumes were clearing, and he felt the best he had since Lamu. It was still hard to shake the image of Esther, diamonds spewing from her mouth, but the thought that he was actually taking concrete steps to avenge her energized him.

• • •

The apartment was in one of the many anodyne milk-carton high-rises that had sprung up around the UN. Tshishkedi opened the door almost before the bell had finished ringing and waved Martin into the spacious apartment.

How the other half lived, Martin thought, complete with stunning river views of the East River, which stretched all the way from the Triborough down past Hell Gate to the Midtown Bridge. It was a brilliantly sunny day, and Martin found the constant traffic of barges and tugs relentlessly crisscrossing the choppy waters somehow soothing.

"*Bienvenue*, Martin. Anything to drink?"

"*Mais non*," Martin slipped effortlessly into French.

"I trust everything went well at the consulate."

"Exactly as I expected, right down to the expedite fee."

"Eh bien, somethings are what they are in my country as well as many others. What starts at the top must always go to the bottom. It is gravity, mon amie." The remark was offered without the slightest hint of apology. Sadly, it said everything. "So where do we start, Monsieur Fine?"

"At the beginning for a beginner. Who do I want to know? Who do I *not* want to know? What's the general background in Kinshasa as to how many enquiring minds are around? All that good stuff."

Tshishkedi gave him an appraising glance that said much but revealed less. "The situation in Kinshasa is relatively relaxed right now. Mobutu is secure. Most are preoccupied with the fight and making sure there are no problems."

"Eh bien, I'll be just another face in the crowd."

"Yes, as long as you are discreet. I will make sure that the right, wrong people are selected for your minders. We will need a good cover for you, of course, and I have been thinking about that. It must be something that allows you to meet some of the more interesting types in the ville."

"For sure. It won't be five minutes if I'm doing anything useful that they'll figure out that I'm not the normal mzungu over for the fight."

"*Certainement*, so you must be somehow involved in smuggling, but shall we say something far removed from the items we are concerned about? It really should be only one thing: diamonds."

"Given my history, that's a good fit and would allow me to mingle with the right folks."

"Yes, it will also fit if anyone figures out who you really are. Your previous efforts were not completely unknown to us or others who might take an interest."

"That did give me some concern. Not sure where the diamonds ended up or who might have been pissed about it. As per usual, the major was suitably tight-lipped about it. 'Don't concern yourself. I sorted it.' Famous last words, not that I cared at the time."

"That fact shouldn't surprise any of us. The major is, as you know, usually three steps ahead of everyone else. I believe that he somehow came into possession of the stones and redistributed them more equitably."

"Meaning . . . ?"

"Some for all of the interested parties, as well as perhaps some for his retirement fund. Having unlisted assets does allow one a certain flexibility of actions that official budgets do not."

Martin was dying to know who the interested parties were and if Tshishkedi was one of the same—but way too smart to ask. If he got an answer, it would be BS. And the only one less likely than Tshishkedi to tell him anything useful would be the major.

"How likely is it that someone besides you in the security world over there will spot me?"

"Possible, hence the cover story. The real fear, of course, is if some of your old acquaintances from the Amis hear that you are there."

"I presume that you know who they were?" It was a stupid question, and Martin knew the minute he finished the sentence.

"You know enough to know that Shaba is of particular interest to us. Unfortunately, in this case, it is of interest to everyone with an interest in Zaire."

"So where do I start in Kinshasa?"

"At your hotel. I think it is best if we chum the water a little and see what comes to you. I will spread the bait out in some of the normal places, *et voila*, they will soon come to you. If you start blundering about, it will attract way too much attention from the wrong people."

"So," Martin said, summarizing everything he'd heard so far, "I just check in and let it happen."

Tshishkedi shrugged eloquently and ushered him to the door, and that was that.

• • •

Martin was packed and ready to go that evening. Said it all about his life, he thought ruefully. Rootless. Skin deep. He owed the major a favor and said so when he called him at his hotel for any last-minute instructions.

"Nonsense, Martin. You're the right choice for this on every level. Besides, you may not be thanking me a few weeks from now."

Martin didn't dwell on the major's last remark as he headed to the airport to catch the overnight flight to Kinshasa. He wondered if he would look back on the trip as a rejuvenation or the continuation of a nightmare.

It was a long, tedious flight, but Martin had plenty to occupy his thoughts as he drifted in and out of sleep. The same nightmarish collage: Russell leering as Mapende bled out, with a dash of Bagaza's manic death mask layered over top for added effect. Every time he had the dream he felt disappointed that he wasn't strangling Russell instead of Bagaza—not that the latter hadn't thoroughly deserved to die. Martin hadn't lost a single night's sleep over terminating him.

He woke up in sweat-drenched clothes as the pilot announced the final approach to Ndodo Kinshasa's airport.

Martin might not have been to Kinshasa before, but he was at home the minute the overwhelming humidity wrapped itself around him like a familiar blanket and that familiar fetid scent of rotting vegetation commingled with burning wood smoke and other less savory odors assailed his nostrils.

Surprisingly, no dash was required to get through formalities.

"That surely won't last," he muttered to himself, chuckling mirthlessly

Maybe they were on their best behavior for the fight crowds. That notion was dispelled as soon as he approached the cab rank. He laughed off the first offers, all of them aimed at tourist mzungus, and proceeded down the rank, parrying the shouted entreaties in French.

Finally, toward the end of the line a suitably scrofulous-looking driver gave him a gap-toothed grin. "*Un demi! Un Demi!*"

Half, half. Much closer to what the stewardesses had told him it should cost.

"*D'accord.*" Martin nodded his assent and lobbed his bag into the back of the vintage Peugeot—or Pigeot, as it was known locally. "*L'Intercontinental, s'ils vous plais.*"

"*Monsieur, a l'instant.*" The driver expertly navigated his way out of the chaotic logjam.

This one might have potential, Martin thought. He was going to need a dependable—well, at least *somewhat* dependable—driver to get him around. From what the maps had shown, Kinshasa boasted some large, reasonably well-organized sections—colonial, no doubt—but the newer bits were the prototypical post-colonial hodgepodge of slums, markets formal and informal, and some better housing for expats and wealthy locals. To his surprise, Martin spotted several greenswards too. On his own, it would take years and lots of wasted time to find his way around without help. He didn't have either.

"*Comment epelez vous.*"

"Hippolyte Shaba, *a votre service.*"

"Looking for a good job?" Martin tried in Swahili. Though most of the Kinois spoke Lingala or French, some also spoke Baswahili, a dialect of the Kiswahili with which Martin was familiar.

"*Missouri Sana, Bwana.* I, Hippolyte, will be your driver, your friend, your guide."

"*Missouri, rafiki*, you will be pleased with me, I assure you."

"Two hundred US a week, *va bien?*"

Martin figured this was going to be a three-language sympathy.

French, Swahili, English—whichever of the three was used would do. It was an outrageous sum, but he was playing with house money, and he figured it was more than the Surete or whatever they were called these days was paying him.

"*Monsieur tu es un vrai miracle.* Whatever you want, require, or wish for—it is yours."

Including my wife and first-born, Martin thought, chuckling to himself. "Let's make sure you're worth every penny, Hippolyte."

"It can only be that way, monsieur."

"It's Trent. How is the crime here? Do I have to be very careful?"

"A few weeks ago, perhaps. Not now. The president arrested one thousand local criminals about a month ago. He put them in cells below the Stade De Mai and had one executed publicly every day for one hundred days. Kinshasa is very safe right now, as he wanted it for the big fight."

Straight out of Amin's playbook, Martin thought to himself. Time to get serious. In the land of the "Big Man," there was rarely any margin for error. The dry, acidic taste of adrenalin surged through his mouth, and goddammit, he loved it. Loved it too much.

"Eh bien, Monsieur Trent, we are here."

"Thanks, Hippolyte. Please give me an hour or so, and then pick me up. I'd like a little familiarization tour."

It never failed to amaze Martin how Intercontinentals always looked the same the world over: absolutely devoid of any local flavor. In a perverse way, he thought, that was their charm, present company accepted.

Check-in was quick. The lobby wasn't buzzing with too many fight types yet—perhaps unfortunate from a camouflage point of view. Martin was shown to a nice suite on the top floor with great views. He glanced out a large picture window and spotted the lights of Congo-Brazzaville glittering across the river. Different country, and completely different-looking city.

The major clearly had a big expense account for this one—something to be subtly enquired about. Not that it was likely to get him anywhere, but he loved to study the major's obfuscation techniques.

Showered and in his tropical clothes, he was downstairs in time to sample a frosty Castel, the excellent local lager, before going outside to find his driver. "Hippolyte, just drive me around and show me the important areas to know. Everything business, government, and most important, entertainment."

"Certainly, Mr. Trent. Am I to assume that you might want some company?" Hippolyte's tone was innocent, his grin wolfish.

"Certainly, but not now. I also want to see places where I might encounter interesting business opportunities. I've often found that business and pleasure can be found in the same place."

"This is true, but also other types can be found there."

"D'accord. Your job will be to help me sort the proverbial wheat from the chaff." This was where things would get interesting, Martin thought to himself, but it was an excellent opportunity to establish himself as on the make but in search of relatively unthreatening opportunities—plus size up the scene.

The tour was enlightening, if only because Hippolyte gave Martin an idea of the scope of Kinshasa. It had grown from a sleepy colonial capital of less than 500,000 to a sprawling urban agglomeration of 1.5 million in a little more than ten years. Parts of it, especially La Cite, provided a textbook example of unplanned urban sprawl.

The slums the world over all had one characteristic, Martin thought as he hastily rolled up his window to avoid the stench: they served as a perverse tribute to man's ability to survive. Sad but true. An affirmation of life amidst the detritus of society. The hollow-eyed inhabitants wandered about, zombie automatons doing the bare minimum to get by.

"*Dur*, Monsieur Trent, and still they come."

"But why? Surely they would be better off staying in the country. At least there's food."

"Not always, mon ami. Up country may look green, but it is not always edible green. There are no jobs, mon ami. Unemployment in the country is eighty percent, in Kinshasa forty percent."

"Surely there must be jobs after Mobutu nationalized everything."

"One would think, but *non*. When Mobutu drove out all the business owners, there were no Zairians with the ability to run the businesses, so they soon failed."

"What about copper, diamonds, etc.?"

"They do not fall far from Nsele."

"Nsele?"

"President Mobutu's compound."

"I'd like to see that at some point."

"It is far, and you must have a reason to be around there."

"Figures. So where are we going this evening?"

"The casino, I think. It is popular these days. *Tout le monde* visits there."

•••

When they pulled up to the sprawling complex in an upscale hotel, Martin agreed with Hippolyte's choice. The mostly well-dressed crowd of Congolese and expats streamed in and out through the doors.

"Looks like a good place to get the feel of things, Hippolyte. Will you come in with me?"

"*Mais non*, monsieur."

To be pursued later, Martin thought as he got out. "Give me about ninety minutes to explore. I won't be super long. I'm tired from the flight."

The casino was no more, no less than Martin had expected. *Close your eyes*, he thought, *and you could have been in London or Paris—or more relevantly here, Brussels*. The place was packed with about a fifty/fifty split between locals and expats. Kinshasa might have been poor, but there was no evidence of its poverty here. Large piles of chips exchanged hands rapidly.

Martin decided to head over to the bar for a ringside seat.

A striking woman approached him a short while later. She was attractive in an interesting fashion: clearly not purely Bantu or Nilo Hamitic, high cheekbones, café au lait coloring. "Baker," she said, "it's been too long, vraiment." Her perfume wafted over him before she finished the sentence. She kissed him lightly on each cheek. "Aren't you going to offer an old friend a drink?"

"What else can a gentleman do? What would you like?"

"Champagne, of course. Is there anything else to drink at the casino?"

He signaled the waitress. "But of course. I'm afraid my memory has failed me. Your name?"

"Really, Mr. Fine, that was not what I was told."

Martin grappled with the statement. Somehow, he wasn't surprised at how quickly he'd been tagged. The good news was he wasn't being beaten up in some Garde Civile hellhole. "Always glad to buy an attractive lady a glass of champagne. Even better when I know her name."

"Chlothilde Dupasse," she said with a smile. "My employer said you are fond of African women."

"Is your employer a certain British gentleman?"

"Perhaps." The smile was charming. The tone did not invite further questions. "I am to be your guide to all things Zairois. If you do not know your way around, Kinshasa can be a dangerous place."

"Bien sur. Are we going to be here for a while, or do you have something else in mind?"

"There is another boite that I think we should visit. There are usually interesting people there. It is not far, and your driver will certainly know it."

• • •

If Hippolyte was surprised to see Martin emerge from the casino with an attractive woman in tow less than thirty minutes after entering, he didn't show it. "Where to Monsieur, et . . ." He paused none too subtly for effect. ". . . Mademoiselle?"

"*L'ambasadeur*, Hippolyte."

"*A votre service.*"

Another joker in the pack, Martin thought to himself. This was getting interesting fast.

Chlothilde touched him lightly on the leg. "Baker, you have selected well. Hippolyte is known to us. He has no current affiliation, and he is no friend of the regime."

"D'accord." He knew she was only going to give him info if and when she chose to. She'd been trained by the major too. Or was it Tshishkedi? Or both? "Are we going to meet anyone in particular at this club?"

"Perhaps. We will have some champagne and see what develops." The smile was charming and completely studied.

He sank into the upholstery as her scent wafted over him. Jet lag was kicking in, and it was too dark outside to make out much. Fortunately for him, the ride was quick, or he would have nodded off.

The Ambassadeur looked like the swankest boite in Kinshasa after the casino. The crowd looked similar too. The doorman smiled as he greeted Chlothilde, and the captain hustled them over to a prime table next to the dance floor that magically appeared out of nowhere.

"They seem to know you well."

"I have been here a few times. It is *assez charmante mais cher*."

That was for sure. Five hundred dollars for a mediocre bottle of champagne. *Pre-fight markup*, Martin thought to himself.

"Ah, the lovely Chlothilde." A handsome African in a very expensive suit—and the now seemingly de rigueur diamond cufflinks—politely kissed her hand before turning to Martin. "Justin Devreaux, at your service. I am the owner."

"Nice to meet you. Looks like you have the hot spot in town." Martin extended his hand. "Trent Baker."

Devreaux shook it firmly. "It is never dull here, often entertaining, sometimes even stimulating."

They sure did like the throwaway teaser lines in these parts, Martin thought.

"And what, if I may ask, are you here for, Monsieur Baker? The fight perhaps?"

"Call me Trent. I like visiting interesting places when interesting things are happening. One never knows what opportunities might pop up."

"The biggest boxing match in history is not required for things to be interesting in Kinshasa, as I am sure you will find out. You have made a good start with your guide. The charming Chlothilde knows the right people and places to discover most things of interest. As you are new here and have been presented by a mutual friend, may I offer you lunch tomorrow?"

"Sounds wonderful."

A half hour later, Martin was pretty much done and figured the scripted part of the evening had played out. Much was obvious. The only thing missing was the author of the piece. He could hardly keep his eyes open.

"Eh bien, Martin, you are falling asleep with a beautiful lady sitting next to you. Let us get you back to the hotel." Chlothilde's lips lightly brushed his cheek. "Come. We will have other nights."

Martin decided to let that one ride. He'd be a fool not to be interested—and an even bigger one to rush his fences. "Will you come to lunch tomorrow?"

"*Mais non*. That is for you and Justin to talk."

The drive back was a blur, as was the gentle kiss on the cheek she gave him at the hotel.

"Here is my number," she said. "Call me after your lunch with Justin."

CHAPTER

5

As he lay in bed the next morning, Martin tried to parse the previous day's events. Obviously, with the possible exception of Hippolyte, everything had been scripted, but by whom and for whom? One thing was for sure: he'd been on the ground less than twenty-four hours, and already his cover was blown all to hell. As always, more would be revealed—the ever-present state of affairs in Africa. Was today's movie going to be a drama, comedy, or nightmare?

Hippolyte dropped him off at l'Ambassadeur about one o'clock. Martin was struck by the club's almost forlorn feel in the daylight. All clean, chairs stacked neatly on the table—it was sterile and devoid of charm.

"All dressed up and no place to go, as the agnostic put on his gravestone."

"Eh bien, Trent, how are you settling in?"

"So far so good, Justin, but what can a man see or know in thirty-six hours?"

"Vraiment, not enough time for him to see much, but perhaps enough time for him to be seen." Justin was dressed more casually—the slick veneer of the night before having disappeared—but

26

he still maintained a suave but cautious air. "A common friend called me from New York yesterday. We had an interesting chat."

"So you know why I'm here?"

"Yes, I have already tossed a few pebbles into the pond. Like most places, Kinshasa is big in numbers but small in certain circles. In some ways, I am surprised about our mutual friend's concern. In others, not."

"Yes, it could be a tricky situation. Very hard to tell who's who and wants what."

"Right on one count, wrong on the other. We know what they all want."

"So I make like a fight tourist and schmooze around for a few days."

"For now, yes, but if the people I suspect are involved actually are, it will not be long before you are approached. In the meantime, should you need anything, do not hesitate to contact me. I have been instructed to help you."

• • •

After an amiable lunch, Martin headed back to the hotel, wondering about next steps. The lobby was heaving with an influx of obvious fight types, which made it easier for him to blend in—not that he really wanted to. The tourists were an advertisement for "Ugly Americans" abroad.

The concierge waived him over. "Monsieur Baker, an envelope was left for you." He handed him a worn, grubby envelope.

Martin resisted the urge to open it after stepping inside the elevator. As soon as the door closed, he opened it.

Come to 48 Avenue Bataille at 16:00 this afternoon.

The writing was a scrawl—either a disguise or from a semi-illiterate. It didn't leave him any choice but to go. It was what he was there for. Besides, he wasn't deep enough into anything to be concerned.

...

Hippolyte was concerned about the neighborhood and told him so.

As they pulled up, Martin could see why. The buildings were what he would have called "crumbling colonial." They'd all seen better days—at least fifty years' worth. Number 48 had been an ochre-yellow at one point, but the combination of peeling paint and cracked plaster made it look like a popped pimple.

Martin pushed open the flimsy door and found himself in a dark, dingy room that obviously was an illegal nightclub. Battered tables were spaced haphazardly facing a primitive plywood bar. The place reeked of stale beer, staler bodies, and tobacco.

Two large men stared at him without expression. He'd seen this movie before.

He walked up to the bar, ordered a cold Primus, and then sat down to see what would happen next.

Just as he was wiping off the top of the Primus bottle—48 Avenue Bataille was definitely a drink-from-the-bottle kind of place—the door opened, and a dapper African slid into the chair opposite him.

He looked as out of place as Martin felt and nodded at the muscle next door. "Monsieur Baker, I must apologize for the cryptic nature of the note and the somewhat off-the-beaten-path meeting place. The hotels are swarming with all sorts of people we wouldn't necessarily want observing our meeting. Allow me to introduce myself. I am Boniface Katanga." He was short, squat, and muscular. He was also carrying and made no attempt to close his ill-fitting suit jacket.

Point made, Martin thought to himself. "You might be right about the hotel clientele, but I can't be sure until you tell me why I've been summoned here."

"Word has reached me and my associates through irregular channels that you are interested in certain goods." Boniface didn't look like the sort of guy who used regular channels.

"Perhaps. Or just as interested in other people who are interested." Martin knew asking Boniface anything about himself or his employers was useless at this point. The field seemed to be growing all the time, and in all likelihood, many were double-dipping.

"But of course. These things always work both ways. I am surprised you haven't heard more. My sources say it is the Amis who are interested."

"In what, specifically?"

"Things that come from the ground and go tick-tick."

"Really? I thought those assets were already controlled by the government and its partners, who last time I looked were the Amis." Martin was rapidly recalibrating—and wondering if there was anyone in Kinshasa who knew less than he did.

"Supposedly, yes, but there are Amis, and there are Amis. Sometimes they are not so similar."

"Do you have anything to back that up, or is it just idle chat, looking for cash?"

"The rumors are persistent from several sources."

"If any of this is true, I can't be the only one interested."

"Vraiment, but you may be the only one who can make inquiries without upsetting certain parties."

Well, Martin thought, that was worth the price of admission. Boniface had to be from the government and no doubt had been put up to him by Tshishkedi. Otherwise, he would have pitched

Martin to buy what was on offer—or at least information about it. Still, it remained to be seen what the major was playing at. Martin knew him too well to assume things were as simple as he'd claimed in New York.

"Am I to suppose that your employers are supportive of subtle enquiries into what may or may not be going down? I'm presuming that's why you had me meet you at this place, whatever it is."

"Yes, of course. We are putting word out that there is an Ami looking about for these types of goods."

Martin studied Boniface. He'd gone inscrutable—something Africans often did when they wanted mzungus to see right through them without learning anything. Martin knew better than to pursue things much further. *Great*, he thought. *The proverbial goat in the trap. Bait for the leopard.* One last dig. "What if the good guys turn out to be the bad guys?"

"Quite possible. Then we will have to arrange a small surprise for them."

"And just how do I figure into this little charade?"

"You will be the transportation expert. I have been told that you have some expertise in that area. In any event, we will help you to look the part. I have also been told to tell you that you will not regret helping us in this little matter."

"Won't they have their own resources?"

"Not if it is who we think it is. They will not be able to use their normal networks."

True enough, Martin thought. Then again, if it was who he thought it was, they weren't going to be too happy to see him, either. Time to trust the major, but he really wished he knew what that enigma wrapped in a riddle was thinking more often. "So, Boniface, I head back to the hotel and make like a fight tourist?"

"*Exactement.*" He shook Martin's hand, flashing the pistol once more, and ushered him to the door. "Patience. I am sure it won't be long before our friends contact you."

Maybe, Martin thought as he signaled Hippolyte over from the curb, but it was hard for him not to want to observe the major's advice for being stuck: "Well, old cock, just go out and start shaking the branches and see what bloody well falls out."

Speaking of which, he mused on the way back to the hotel, where was the old bastard, and what was he up to? The only thing that was for sure was that no one would know until the major was ready. Best to remember he wasn't in charge.

The good news was that he knew and accepted that fact. He wasn't so sure about the other players in the script. Jesus. It wasn't even six. Things were moving fast.

CHAPTER

6

MARTIN WAS BARELY through the hotel doors when he spotted Chlothilde in the bar off the lobby. It was jammed with fight types even though the big event was ten days away. They might have been good cover, but there were times he wished that he was anything but American. "Chlothilde, I'm surprised to see you here. I see you're slumming it."

"*Peut t'etre*. I should ask our employer for danger money, present company excepted."

"I suspect it wouldn't get you very far." He signaled the waiter. "Champagne?"

"Is there anything else? But really, I am not here to drink champagne, though it's nice of you to order it. I have a message for you."

"Do tell."

"Your friend said to tell you that someone you know will be here soon. He said you will not be happy, but the person will not be surprised to see you. Your friend also told me to tell you that it's all part of the plan."

"I'd feel better if I had a remote idea of what the plan was."

"Really—"

"I'll know when I need to," he said, finishing her sentence for her.

They both laughed.

"Have you had dinner yet?" Martin asked.

"Mais non, is that an invite?"

"Could be. I'll buy—if you take me to the right place. Not a tourist dive, either. Something *tout a fait Zairois.*"

• • •

Chez Flore was tout a fait Zairois: loud, joyous, and busy. The staff obviously knew Chlothilde. The captain waved her to the front of the queue and hustled them over to an empty two-top that appeared out of nowhere.

"Nice to be known."

"My uncle is the owner, which is a good thing, or we would have waited a long time. Sometimes it is over an hour."

"You do seem to get around a bit. I'm thinking I'm lucky to have met you—or I guess I should say, to have been introduced to you."

"Maybe. Let's see how you feel in a few more days."

Or a few hours, Martin thought to himself.

Chlothilde turned out to be a deep well. Obviously from a well-connected family, she had studied in France. She was a bit vague about the family business and her position in it, but then again, he wasn't being very forthcoming about his background. Somehow, he sensed that she knew a lot more about him than he did her, but then again, just about everyone involved seemed to, he thought.

The dinner was delicious. They danced to the loud but lilting Congolese. She was lithe and sensual but also somehow ambivalent, leaving Martin unsure of his footing. He wasn't certain what he wanted to do. He was still pretty raw emotionally from his last encounter with an African woman. He was definitely attracted to Chlothilde. She was much more sophisticated than Esther had been, but he sensed she, too, was holding back, which was a relief. The last time he'd mixed business with pleasure, it hadn't worked out so well.

Hippolyte dropped him at the hotel on the way to drop off Chlothilde. She gently brushed his lips, leaving a taste of champagne and perhaps just the hint of something to come.

• • •

Martin's sleep was troubled. Jumbled images of the beach and the blood diamonds played out over and over. Not for the first time, he woke in entangled, sweat-drenched sheets.

Enough already, he thought as he showered.

It was early by Congolese and tourist standards when he strolled into the empty dining room for breakfast. He sipped his double, wondering what the day had in store. It was time to observe the major's primary dictum about shaking the bloody trees. Always good advice, but which trees?

"Well, Mr. Fine—or should I say Baker?—a little bird told me you might be around in these parts."

Fuck. It was Agent Russell, complete with walrus mustache and oozing affability. As if nothing had happened between them.

Martin was stunned. He'd always figured that this was going to happen but hadn't prepared himself for what he would do when it did.

At least the bastard didn't offer his hand. "Cat got your tongue?"

"You know I rehearsed in my mind a hundred times what I would say and do when I next saw you. Now I'm just numb."

"Just as well. It wouldn't pay to try anything stupid."

True enough, Martin thought. He scanned the large empty

room and saw only one other table occupied. The three large Africans seated around it didn't remotely resemble tourists or local businessmen.

"Okay, Russell, I guess I'm not really all that surprised to see you. Plenty of US interest around here. I see you brought an insurance policy with you."

"True, Mobutu is our boy these days, but things can change rapidly around here, as you know. I try to be prepared."

"So are we just going to pretend the whole Uganda thing didn't happen?"

"Listen, Martin, you're young. One of the things you're going to have to learn if you're going to play this game is that you have to have a short memory."

Just what he needed: a how-to tutorial from a card-carrying sociopath. "I'll be sure to take that under advisement. I assume you didn't drop by to give me lifestyle advice."

"Just heard from a mutual acquaintance that you were back in Africa and had assembled some useful assets."

"I'm not sure who or what you're talking about."

If that bothered Agent Russell, he gave no sign of it. "That's okay. It's not time to talk yet, but just wanted to touch base and let you know that I'm around and that our interests may coincide at some point. I'll keep you posted. And no hard feelings about the night on Lamu. Shit happens."

"Okay, Russell." What else was there to say?

Agent Russell and his goon squad exited, leaving Martin with a tidal wave of conflicting emotions. He teared up, all the while feeling engulfed in rage. He wouldn't have believed it possible, but there it was. His anger was tinged with guilt and the damming knowledge that he'd played as significant of a role in Esther's death as Katerega and the rest of Russell's goons as had. That was a stain that would never wash out.

Chlothilde interrupted his revery—if he could call it that. "*Mon cher*, you look like you have just seen a ghost."

"Or someone just walked across a grave of someone I was close to."

"Yes, I saw him." She brushed his forearm lightly. "I did warn you."

"About someone, and the major did hint at it, but still, when I saw the bastard in the flesh for the first time . . ."

"*Doucement*, easy. Your chance will come, but it must be cold, *n'est ce pas*."

"For sure. Not that I'm unhappy to see you, but what brings you here so early?"

"Breakfast and a chat, followed by a meeting."

"Rude of me not to offer. I was someplace else." Seeing her so soon after having Esther's death rubbed in his face made him uncomfortable, especially since he was attracted to her.

"Yes, I understand, but for now, that must be over. We have a meeting with someone important as soon as we finish."

They ate somewhat hurriedly, which suited his jangled nerves. Seeing Russell had pulled the cork out of the jug, and now a mysterious important meeting on top of that. What the heck? It wasn't even nine o'clock yet.

• • •

Hippolyte pulled up in front of a shiny new office building about twenty minutes later. Whoever they were about to meet was clearly wealthy and healthy.

Chlothilde seemed to know exactly where she was going. A short elevator ride later, she guided Martin into the offices of Gecamines, the national mining company.

They were ushered into an extremely well-furnished office, and somehow Martin wasn't surprised to see Etienne Tshishkedi seated there. It was like the man been transported from his New York office a few moments earlier. Same dark blue pinstripe shirt. Same huge diamond cufflinks that the Zairois elite seemed to favor.

"Bien venue, Monsieur Fine. And of course, it is always a pleasure to see the beautiful Chlothilde." He kissed her on both cheeks in Gallic fashion before returning his attention to Martin. "May I offer you coffee, tea?"

"I'm fine. Chlothilde?"

"Mais non, Etienne. Why have you summoned us here so early?"

"Obviously, for important reasons, and your uncle is very much aware that we are meeting."

One day soon, Martin thought, he would find out who the mysterious uncle was.

"My uncle is the minister of mining." She smiled as if reading his mind—something that seemed to come naturally to her. "That may make things clearer as we go along. Etienne, continue please."

"So, Monsieur Fine, you might remember our first meeting in New York. I also believe that you had an encounter in the hotel dining room that might have further confirmed our suspicions."

"Our old friend Russell, one of my all-time favorites."

"Quite. Well, would it interest you to know that he is now the chief of station here?"

"Interest and maybe scare the shit out of me—pardon my Anglo Saxon. That bastard has never done anything good in his life."

"To be sure. He must be always watched carefully, which of course we are doing. As is common with these things, it is not always that simple. Presently, he enjoys Mobutu's complete confidence."

"That's unfortunate. The proverbial fox guarding the chicken coop."

"That is what we must prove before he can steal everything."

"So," Martin said, "I presume a trap? With yours truly as the bait?"

"A small part of the bait, but there are bigger prizes than you involved, rest assured."

"Of that I have no doubt. Okay, so I'm in Kinshasa. I've been braced by Russell. Isn't it time you put me a little in the know?"

"I—*we*—would certainly like to, but finding out is going to be a key part of your work. Unfortunately, we don't know any more now than when we spoke a few days ago. However, we may know more soon. We put it about that you are in Kinshasa to buy and smuggle out diamonds and other goods. After all, you do have a bit of a background."

Martin couldn't argue with that. His previous partner's networks had most definitely extended deep into Zaire and equally deeply into the paranoia of its current master. "So maybe Russell was doing more than sniffing around a few hours ago."

"Hopefully he was sniffing around the bait. We are hopeful that he sees you as the last piece in his puzzle. After all, he is way too smart to use any local networks."

"True enough, but I'm going to need a lot more than what I have on tap right now to convince him."

"To be sure, and we are assembling it for you, as we speak. It is a tricky balancing act, as it can't be networks that he uses in his official capacity. Yet if he gets any hint that we are behind it . . ." Etienne's shrug needed no translation.

"Are you sure he has committed to this little extracurricular exercise?"

"Not entirely, but it does fit a pattern. He did a lot of business with your old acquaintance Amin after the unfortunate conclusion of your last escapade."

"Etienne, it wasn't unfortunate from your side of things."

"True, mon ami, and we were on the same side as Russell in that case. Always remember, though: this Africa, and things can change very rapidly. In any case, he is not—how shall I say?—sympatico."

"That's very polite," Martin said, unable to hide the disgust on his face. "Try psychotic and completely dangerous, not to mention homicidal."

Etienne shrugged eloquently. "Normal types rarely work in our area. This time, our interests are aligned elsewhere."

"So. What's next?"

"We start building your network. I have arranged some meetings for you. Some of the more interesting types around town. Chlothilde will, of course, accompany you in case you need translation."

"That's handy for all of us. I've certainly had less attractive minders in my time." Of course, the obvious question was how many different folks she was minding him for. No point in asking that, he figured. All would be revealed—or hopefully at least enough to keep him from getting killed.

Etienne handed him a piece of paper. "Their names and hang-outs are all on this. Chlothilde knows the places, if not the people."

"So are we sticking to the diamonds line, or do I hint at something more exotic?"

"Oh, I think you pass yourself as a man of commerce, open to any opportunities. We are spreading the story of your last adventure. Aka was not unknown, and as you know, the things we are concerned about come from Shaba province also."

"Fair enough." It seemed simple enough, but it never was. "I assume Chlothilde will be the messenger."

Etienne rose and ushered them to the door. "*Oui, mon vieux.*"

• • •

As soon as they were in the car, Martin handed Chlothilde the list. "I assume you're familiar with this?"

"Of course."

"So where do you fit into this appropriately muddy picture?"

"Exactly what do you wish to know?" She delivered the question with a classic blank look.

African women, just like their male counterparts, seemed to have the ability to go blank. A man could look right through them, he thought, and see nothing.

"Who, what, why. I'll leave out where for the time being."

"I have many and no master, depending on the circumstances." She smiled and ran her finger gently across his cheek. "Sometimes, it just depends on the day."

"Charming and enigmatic, but not nearly good enough. I'll need more."

Chlothilde laughed gently, opened her purse, and handed Martin an envelope.

Martin was somewhat surprised to see the major's handwriting.

"He knows you well. He predicted to the minute when you would dig your heels in. Well, go ahead. Read it."

Well, old cock, you're right on schedule. Patience is on the force-feeding menu anon. So I know that you're wondering where all these pieces fit. The good news is that we have the outside of the jigsaw sussed, but the middle needs work. That's your job. Afraid its all a bit muddy right now. This much I can tell you: the only one you are to completely trust until I get there is Chlothilde. Watch the rest of them very carefully. Their agendas shift by the day. That's all for now. Keep the faith. If things work out right, we'll sort Russell—and I do mean sort him—once and for all and be home in time for dinner, so to speak.

Martin laughed to himself. The note was pure Major. He could almost visualize the facial expressions that would have accompanied it if it the words been spoken. It told him everything he wanted to know and nothing he needed to learn.

"He is very fond of you, you know."

"And I he. Not that the note leaves me any clearer, except that I can trust you, which is encouraging, if true. So . . . truth or dare time. What is your connection to him?"

"He and my father are very close friends. He saved my father's life during the whole Katanga affair. I am his goddaughter. It might interest you to know that he looks upon you as a godson."

That pleased him, but he didn't know what to say. "So what next?"

"Some lunch at my house, if you wish."

• • •

Her villa sat in Gombe, and it didn't take Martin long to figure out that it must have been incredibly expensive. The old masks hanging from the walls looked priceless alongside contemporary pieces that wouldn't have looked out of place in any New York or London gallery.

"There's a suit you can borrow in the bedroom to the right. I thought a swim before lunch would be refreshing. We will eat beside the pool."

How the other half live, Martin thought as they sat down to a lunch of roasted fish in banana leaves accompanied by an expensive French wine. "What was it you said your family did again?"

"Touche, the major said you come from money too." She was good.

"Finance, and they might be rich, but I'm not."

"My father has many interests: mining, banking, and others. He is close to Mobutu."

That connected several dots for him.

"Well, Martin, you have nothing to say. I have not known you for long, but you are rarely without words. Come. Let's go somewhere we don't need any." She took him by the hand and led him inside.

CHLOTHILDE DROPPED HIM at the hotel at five o'clock. "Martin, I will be here at eight. We will have dinner and go shake some trees as my godfather would say." She brushed his cheeks lightly with her lips. "Also, the dessert this afternoon was not part of the assignment."

Food for thought as he rode the crowded lift up to his floor. He really liked Chlothilde, and obviously she felt the same way about him. But he couldn't shake the fear that if he got too involved, the same thing would happen to her that had happened to Esther. That said, she was in it up to her immaculately coiffed corn rows.

Judging by the garish clothes and the stench from well-chewed, cheap cigars, the fight crowd was arriving. Martin cringed inwardly. Cultural shame by association was always a hard pill to swallow.

He breathed a sigh of relief when he got to his room. He needed a cold shower, beer, and time to think in that order.

No such luck.

He cursed softly after hearing a knock on the door. "Who's there?"

"Jack Walls, a friend of your family's."

"You're going to have to do a lot better than that," Martin said. "Are you with Russell?"

"Nope. Your father sent me. They're worried about you."

Martin peered through the eyehole in the door.

Walls, a plump mzungu with red hair, was straight out of Hollywood central casting and looked wilted in his pinstripe suit. Only problem was they were in equatorial Africa, not the back lot at Paramount Studios in California.

"No shit, Shylock," Martin finally replied. "I'm worried about myself. ID under the door. That's not a request."

A passport and another document slid under the door. Martin perused them and opened the door. "They haven't talked to me in months. They're no doubt suffering terminal embarrassment from my last trip, not that they could have heard much."

"Your father is connected. They know the gist of it."

Martin very much doubted that anyone involved in the Uganda caper was going to be talking much about it. It was so like his family to not appear to give a shit and then get religion at the worst conceivable time. They'd probably gotten just enough of a whiff of things to want to get involved, no doubt out of concern for scandal, not his wellbeing.

"Do you have the remotest idea of what you're stepping into? Have you worked in Africa before?"

"Well, no, but I have worked in some tough places stateside."

"Oh boy, I hope they're paying the shit out of you. Brother, you have absolutely no clue what you are walking into. My advice would be to call them and say you found me and that I'm fine, charge a hefty fee, and head home—before something bad happens. I have an appointment. Do yourself and me a favor and don't follow me around like a lapdog."

Walls departed, but it was clear to Martin that he hadn't gotten the message.

When Martin left the hotel an hour later, he spotted him immediately on the first side street up from the hotel—FBI surveillance handbook for sure. He wasn't high-grade talent—also for sure. Martin started to approach him when suddenly two large guys in ill-fitting suits surrounded him. They stunk of BO, stale cigarettes, and beer fumes.

Jesus, spare me, he thought. *They all come out after dark.*

"You will walk quietly with us, Mr. Fine."

Martin sized them up quickly. Not well trained. He grabbed the closest one, putting an armlock on him, and slammed him into his partner as he was drawing a knife. The man grunted as the knife plunged into his arm, but Martin wasn't done. With one smooth additional move, he disarmed the knife guy, breaking his arm with a satisfying crack.

"Fuck off and *allez-y*, while you at it."

They staggered off, leaving a trail of blood on the sidewalk.

Martin glanced around. It had all happened so quickly and far enough from the lights of the hotel that no one seemed to have noticed. He wasn't done.

He walked over to Walls. "You've got two choices: you can file a report saying I've acclimatized nicely and am doing well, or I can use my connections to get you deported ASAP. Decide quickly. I'm out of patience, and you're far more likely to get me killed than save me."

Wall grimaced. "Advice taken. I'm way out of my depth here."

"Very true, buddy. There is no bottom here."

Martin made his way back to the hotel and found Hippolyte.

"Monsieur Martin, I saw them following you, but with all the fight people and the traffic, I couldn't get to you."

"*Ca va*. They were amateurs. Please let your superiors know, and make sure that mzungu Walls gets politely deported. He's a stooge and no danger. On to the rest of the night."

Hippolyte waded cautiously through the fight mobs clogging the streets. Fat, florid, perspiring heavily, and wreathed in cheap cigar smoke, the tourists were the prototypical ugly Americans, and there simply was no escaping them. They were exactly as they were supposed to be. In contrast to the rest of the picture. Martin was pensive as they drove into the velvety night. Nothing was ever as it seemed in Africa.

. . .

The Ambassadeur was packed with a distinctly local crowd when Martin and Chlothilde arrived. The captain immediately ushered them to a prime table by the jammed dance floor. A frosty bottle of Tattinger followed immediately.

"Pays to have friends in high places with hefty expense accounts."

Chlothilde smiled. She looked fabulous in a long gown with a light African print and gold embroidery. The whole room seemed to notice as she stood up and kissed him on the cheeks. "Martin, there really is nothing better to drink under these circumstances."

"Mind if I join you? I personally selected this bottle. Only the best for an honored guest." Justin kissed Chlothilde's hand with a Gallic flourish.

Martin had to laugh. Only a Francophone could have pulled it off without looking like an idiot, not that Martin wasn't slightly jealous, truth be told.

"At least the fight crowd hasn't discovered this place yet," he said. "My hotel is teeming with them, and they make my skin crawl."

"I am sure they will be here soon enough, but their money is as good as anyone's. I didn't drop by just to help you drink this excellent champagne, however. It will surely interest you to know that there is a man about town with many varied interests who has expressed interest in meeting you."

"That did not take long," Chlothilde said, laughing. "Having friends in all of the wrong places certainly helps. Justin, who is this man of affairs?"

"Mamadou Diop."

"The name sounds familiar."

"Like many Senegalese, he has a wide net and fingers in many pies, some of which are legal. I will bring him over."

Diop was tall and thin like many of the Senegalese that Martin had encountered. He was expensively tailored with the de rigueur diamond cufflinks and a chunky gold Rolex—a walking cliché for a successful smuggler of the African genus.

"Mamadou Diop at your service." He brushed Clotilde's hand with an air kiss, gave Martin's a firm pump, and slid into the empty seat. "It happens, believe it or not, that we all have some mutual acquaintances."

"Really? Do tell." Martin poured him a glass of champagne.

"I believe you had some dealings with an old acquaintance of mine who sadly is no longer with us: Bertain Aka. Chlothilde, I also know your father."

Martin chuckled ruefully. *So much for my alias.* It seemed like the only people in Kinshasa who didn't know his real name were the fight crew. He wasn't sure whether to laugh or cry, but there wasn't much for it at this point.

"It might interest you to know that Bertain and I were close and trusted associates. I know you saved his life once, and I know all about what happened on Lamu. My sympathies for your loss." He offered a seemingly genuine gesture, patting Martin sympathetically on the shoulder. "Our interests might align more than you believe, but that is a subject that we must discuss somewhere far more discreet."

"Open to suggestion on that," Martin said with a nod. "And Chlothilde—where does she fit in your little scheme?"

"Time will tell, but our other mutual acquaintance always has a plan."

No doubt, Martin thought. This had the major's fingerprints all over it. It had all happened too quickly to be anything else. One other certainty was that the three of them combined knew about 10 percent of what was actually going on. The other sure thing was that every strand of the web that was being woven was as independent of the other as the major could make it.

Always play the long game. Cutouts, old boy. Got to have them, and you can't have too many. The major's planning maxims echoed in Martin's psyche.

"Well, Monsieur Diop, you do know how to bait the hook."

"With any luck, we might be fishing for the same dangerous fish." He finished his champagne and handed them a card with a swish Gombe address. "Lunch tomorrow at one. More will be revealed." With that, he silently disappeared into the crowd.

Martin and Chlothilde danced a couple of sets and took themselves off to their car. It was a silent ride.

"Martin, you are so quiet."

"Lots to digest from a five-minute conversation."

"Vraiment. As he said, more will be revealed."

"Yes, but only the part he knows. It's the parts he doesn't know that might be a lot scarier."

They were silent with their thoughts on the ride back to the hotel. Martin was digesting the whirlwind thirty-six hours. It was a lot from a little, if that was possible.

When they got to the hotel, Chlothilde kissed his cheek demurely. "It has been an interesting day on many levels. Let us see what tomorrow brings. I will be here at noon for our meeting with Diop."

CHAPTER

8

THE DINING ROOM was much more crowded the next morning. It was obviously the fight crowd.

Martin ate quickly and left the hotel for another mini tour before heading to the lunch destination. The Intercontinental was in a touristy part of town. There wasn't much of interest aside from the two minders he seemed to have picked up. That didn't surprise him much. The real question was who they were working for.

The major had always told him to do his homework: "Basic recce, old boy. How do you get in—and more importantly, *out*—if you don't wish to be seen? Learn the routes. Memorize them. You may not have much time to think about it." It wasn't hard. Like all big hotels, the Intercontinental had a whole secondary set of service elevators, corridors, and so forth. It only took him twenty minutes or so and renditions of, "*Pardons, je suis manque* (I am lost)," to get it done. He kicked himself for not having done it already.

Chlothilde was punctual, as always. She looked effortlessly chic in a light blue silk pantsuit that perfectly accentuated her dark skin and lithe figure. She wasn't exactly helping Martin blend in. "This, I think, will be more interesting than any of your previous meetings. I have done some checking, and Monsieur Diop is quite an interesting fellow."

"And what does that mean?"

"It seems that he and your friend Aka were partners on a number of ventures. They were probably the biggest diamond exporters in Zaire."

"Really? So they must also have been keeping the big fellow out at Nsele happy."

"Certainement, until the last deal, which, of course you know about."

"All too well. I'm looking forward to seeing what Diop has to say about that. Much of what happened—and more importantly, *why* it happened—isn't unclear to me. You know the major. I got told what I needed to be told and not much else."

"I do know him," she said with a smile, "and I am sure it was for your protection."

Probably, Martin thought.

• • •

Diop's villa was as opulent as Chlothilde's. Ostentation, meaning he was in with the powers-that-be, was the best policy in Zaire and every other land of the Big Man—until it wasn't.

Diop ushered them into a luxurious office and offered coffee.

Martin admired the tasteful modern African art on the walls. Nice ivory tusks, trimmed in silver, hung side by side. Two large, extremely old intricately carved drums completed the picture.

Diop took a seat at his desk. "So, my friends, where should we start?"

"Maybe at the beginning for a simple American."

"You may have been that when you landed in Kampala a year ago, but you are not that now."

That one hit home. Martin felt a pang. It was so, so true. Lessons learned, he hoped. He was certainly more cautious—but also bitter and a shit-ton more cynical. Just the psychic and body armor a man needed for the Congo. "Miscalculation, ego, arrogance, and the pain that can result from them will grow you up in a hurry. Not to mention accepting your naivete killing someone you loved."

"Well, my friend, funny you should say that. I share your pain, but in my case, it was not so much my fault. I—*we*, in fact—were betrayed by a cynical asshole. Actually, far worse than that. A true sociopath."

"Not Russell." Martin intended sarcasm, but it came out as a bitter croak.

"The same. Bertain and I were more than just business associates. We were very close friends. I knew all about the transaction with you and supported it for the same reasons. I know you saved Bertain's life—all of it, everything."

"So how . . . *why* did Russell and gang get involved?"

"It was just him, not his employers. He came to us. He had found out we had been funneling money to the rebels in Shaba and threatened to turn us in to Mobutu unless we gave him the rebel's share."

"Sounds about right. Obviously, he was freelancing. Why didn't he take it all?"

"Ah, but he did—after he had seen our whole operation. He betrayed us and you. He promised us your life would be spared. Not sure why. Maybe he thought killing an Ami would have needlessly complicated things."

"So in the end, he wanted the stones for himself? He was rogue."

"Yes, and has been for a while, but I do not think the stones were for him alone. Clearly, his employers still don't know. We can't talk about it for the same reasons. But this is a riddle in parts. Chlothilde may have some of the pieces."

"As in the *major*-related ones." She smiled. "All will be revealed when he next sees us. I can say that the reason you are alive, Martin, is a deal he made with Russell."

"Sure would like to have been a fly on the wall for that discussion."

"Me too," Diop said, grinning. "I am also sure that if Chlothilde knows anything about it, we will not hear it."

"Gentlemen, I know nothing besides what I have already shared with you, but one thing I will tell you, which I think you already know, is that the major detests Agent Russell."

Martin nodded. "Okay, so we all want to crap in Russell's bed. What's next?"

"Rumor has it that Agent Russell is setting up a three-way deal. Amin helps him get the diamonds, which he swaps for uranium here and then smuggles that to Libya. Upon arrival, Ghaddafi gives him a big down payment on his retirement fund and ships Amin some arms he has been craving for a while."

"Everybody wins but the good guys," Martin said, "except this is Africa, and there aren't any good guys, just less bad ones."

Diop smiled. "A bit cynical, but sadly true, which brings us to where we are. Some less bad guys trying to fuck a really bad guy. Pardon, Chlothilde."

Chlothilde offered an indifferent shrug. "I have nothing polite to say about that man. I have only met him twice at my fathers'. He made my skin crawl. I assume you have an idea."

"The beginnings of one. Agent Russell will soon be in possession of some weapons-grade uranium, which he will want to transport to Libya. He will need transport."

"Surely you don't think he would trust you," Martin said.

"Of course not, but I have a network—one that is not on the government's radar."

Martin wasn't surprised. Diop and Aka would surely have

been playing both sides against the middle. Who didn't in their business? "So I presume that is where I come in."

"If we play our cards right, even better, we may have a nasty surprise for Agent Russell. That is, after all, why we are here."

"What does that look like?"

"That is where Chlothilde and our common friend come in."

"So," Chlothilde said, "the plan is for the goods to be switched out in transit."

How very smart and how very much like the major, Martin thought. Everyone who counted—Mobutu and themselves—would be happy. And everyone who didn't—namely Gaddafi and Amin—would be competing to take care of Russell. All sides against the middle. Nice, but not easy.

"Easy for all of us to sit here and say. I look forward to hearing the details."

Chlothilde laughed gently. "If there is a plan more specific than what I just said, I am not aware of it. There can be no plan until we know Russell's plan. Part of your job will be to find out what his plan is. How can you transport the goods for him without learning most of the details of how he is going to get them?"

Diop took out a pad and wrote down a note. "Take this to the following address. It is the office of an import/export company that I own. Ask for Joseph Kadenda, the manager. He is expecting you."

"For?"

"Arranging a transaction. We must carefully bait the trap for Agent Russell. He is smart, suspicious, and ruthless."

"As well as homicidal—on a good day. What am I smuggling?"

"What else, given your history, but diamonds?"

"That should fly, all things considered."

"It just so happens that I have a consignment going out in a few days. As far as he is concerned, you will be the owner."

· · ·

Kadenda's office was in a mid-level commercial complex in an older business section of Kinshasa.

At last, Martin thought to himself: *someone who operates without the Big Man's need to keep his face by being in your face.*

The secretary, who actually looked efficient, right down to her severe business dress and horn-rimmed glasses, seated them in the perfunctory waiting area without comment and knocked on the inner office door.

Kadenda, neatly but boringly dressed, entered and waved them in. "I have been expecting you. Monsieur Diop has spoken highly of you. I believe you had some dealings with his former partner, Aka."

"True," Martin replied, "and if he recommends you, it's good enough for me."

"What will you be needing me to transport?"

"Diamonds for the first run. Then perhaps something more valuable but less easy to transport."

"How many and where to?"

"About a kilo. Some cut, some rough. Tripoli, Libya."

If the destination surprised Kadenda, he gave no sign of it. "My standard fee is ten percent. You can bring your own appraiser. I will of course have one, but I am sure that we can come to an agreement."

"I'm sure," Martin said with a tight-lipped smile. "How long will it take to arrange transport?"

"No more than a week. When will you be bringing in the merchandise?"

"I'll let you know tomorrow."

"D'accord. Tomorrow, then."

CHAPTER

9

MARTIN WAS SIPPING his first espresso of the day when Agent Russell sat down uninvited opposite him, disturbing his morning revery. That woke him up a lot faster than the expresso.

Russell was his usual jovial self. "You look like you're surprised to see me again."

It pissed Martin off that the CIA agent always seemed so self-satisfied. Of course, that was easy enough for a card-carrying sociopath with zero empathy. "And you look better on a full stomach. Now that we have that out of the way, to what do I owe this distinct pleasure?"

"Just a little check-in with my favorite transportation entrepreneur."

"Do tell."

"Little birdies around town are chattering. Seems someone might be moving some bright shiny things soon."

"Really, so why tell *me*?"

"Because it's rumored to be a mzungu, and you're the only mzungu I know around here that likes to smuggle diamonds."

"Okay. So?"

"So this time, if you are, I don't really give a fuck as long as they aren't financing commie guerillas in Shaba."

"You know I'm pretty short on details—almost as short as you are at this point. Why are we having this extremely hypothetical conversation?"

"For once, our interests might be aligned."

"That's a fucking scary thought. Tell me about it."

Russell glanced around the mostly empty dining room before continuing. "I just might need some specialized transport."

"Come on. You have your own networks—tons of them."

"Yes, but those are for official purposes."

"Now I *am* interested. Is little Mr. Russell contemplating something naughty? That would be worth hearing about."

"Possibly. Everyone has to start retirement planning sometime."

Martin studied Russell's red mop of hair and didn't spot a single strand of gray. "You don't look that old to me."

"Well, a man has got be ready to take advantage of opportunities at any age."

Martin couldn't believe his ears. Only Russell would waste time on such BS while talking to someone who knew what a prime bastard he was. "So am I to assume your present employers are ignorant of this soon-to-be new line of business?"

"Actually, not so new. Lots of water under the bridge since Lamu. So far, though, these transactions have been a discreet little side show."

"So is this a spec conversation, or is there something in the works?"

"If it wasn't close, why would I be speaking to you?"

"In that case, what's the timeline? Hints on the materials."

"More will be revealed, when needed. Also, I'm going to let your next little shipment go ahead unhindered as a peace offering after Lamu." Russell rose and took himself off.

At least he didn't hold out his hand for a shake, Martin thought. *Jesus, as if a few diamonds could ever make up for Mapende. What a tone-deaf asshole.* But in his line of work, a man had to be. It hadn't taken long for the shark to take the bait—or at least sniff it. Martin wondered how soon the great white—as in, the major—would pitch up.

The lobby was awash with press, assorted hangars-on, and other fight-related types when Martin left the dining room. It didn't take long to see why. A squad of Surete types entered the main entrance and formed a phalanx around a portly African American with an impossibly high gray Afro. A chocolate ice cream sundae topped with a Brillo pad instead of a cherry.

Don King, live and in the flesh—lots of it perspiring heavily. He was kitted in a ghetto-red silk satin suit that would have looked absurd on anyone else but fitted his persona perfectly. Martin had seen him bloviating on TV too many times not to instantly recognize him. How could he resist the biggest prize fight of all time being co-promoted by two of the biggest hustlers of all time—Mobutu and Don King? He couldn't have made it up if he tried, and no one would have believed him if he had.

With nothing better to do, he followed the mob into the ballroom. Whatever happened, it was going to be a show for sure.

The goon squad hustled King up to a brightly lit dais surrounded by cameramen. Looked like everything was in place for a real spectacle. Martin had to snatch a child holding an autograph book and whisk him out of their path. There was no getting between King and a microphone.

King sipped on a glass of water and flicked the mic a few times and then got right into it. "Ladies and gentlemen of the press, thank you one and all for coming out today. First, I want to assure you that the greatest fight in the history of the world will be going ahead on schedule in one week's time. No injuries this time. Just the real deal. The Rumble in the Jungle."

King was ducking, weaving, and jiving like the old days when he was running numbers on the ghetto streets. Martin had to admire his sheer nerve and bombast. The old Chuck Berry line about "campaign shouting like a Southern diplomat" came to mind. The press was eating it up, and why not? But everyone knew he was just the warmup for the main act.

"Now I know y'all are waiting for Muhamad and George. There a comin' soon."

As if on cue, a motorcade screamed to a halt outside the hotel entrance and paused theatrically for effect, allowing the mob to almost trample Martin in their hurry to witness the grand entrance. A chauffeur sprinted around the huge Cadillac and opened the door. A pair of massive tree trunks that passed for legs incongruously clad in white boxing shoes slid out slowly and then straightened. It was George Foreman.

Martin was in the back of the scrum, but Foreman was so big Martin could still see most of his upper torso over the crowd.

The crowd parted as Foreman, surrounded by his handlers, strode into the ballroom and mounted the dais.

Foreman was scowling, or maybe that was his permanent expression. He was so big he made King look small. The questions started. They weren't of much interest to Martin. He had heard that Ali and Foreman weren't doing press together. He'd have paid to see Ali, but Foreman was boring, monolithic, and for all that, frightening, like an emotionless robot, a killing machine. Martin hoped Ali had a plan besides bullshit and bravado. They weren't going to be nearly enough. Foreman cast such a visceral aura of raw, animal savagery that Martin could see why so many of his opponents had melted in front of him.

Chlothilde was sauntering in just as Martin emerged from the ballroom. "I didn't know you were interested in the fight."

"A little," Martin said with a shrug. "I love Ali, but it's hard to see him beating that guy at his age."

"Unless Ali has magic, and I believe he has."

"Hope so. It would restore what little faith I have in Karma."

She caressed his cheek. "So bitter at such a young age."

"Life's tough lessons. I hope you never have to understand that."

"I may already know more than you think on that subject."

"Let's compare notes one day. Any reason for this pleasant surprise?"

"Meeting with Diop. It seems our friend has taken the bait."

"Well at least he's interested—in his own nasty way. You're right: This could get real in a hurry. So I assume Diop has a plan."

"We shall soon see."

• • •

Diop had his game face on as he ushered them out onto the terrace, where a glass table had been set for lunch.

Martin noticed the Waterford crystal and fine Sevres porcelain. Just beyond the terrace, well-manicured gardens ran toward a large fountain surrounded by pink and purple bougainvillea.

Diop motioned for them to sit. "Your chat with Kadenda went well, I heard."

"The skids had been well and truly greased," Martin replied, "but there were a few flies around. Two things that always attract flies are diamonds and shit. Unfortunately, this time the shit came in the form of Russell ruining my breakfast this morning. I know it's probably part of the plan, but he's as cold a fish as I have ever encountered."

"We cannot insult the crocodile while our feet are still in the water. An old African proverb—very apropos in this case."

"So the asshole had the nerve to say that since this transaction didn't involve Shaba, he was prepared to overlook his usual commission as a payback for Lamu."

"If the Gods are fair, his time will come later. Did he say anything else?"

"That if this went well, there might be bigger things to come."

"Good. He is not hooked yet but is playing with the bait. We will have to be very careful, as you know."

Martin frowned in acknowledgment. "So one thing I *am* curious about: why Tripoli? Libya seems off the normal track."

"You're right, and they will be going on to other locations, but your associates thought it was important that we demonstrate that we can get things in and out of Libya. One can only assume that as always, he has good reason."

Martin was beginning to connect the dots, and the picture was becoming distressing. Russell wouldn't give Ghaddafi the missing pieces to nukes, would he? Martin needed only a millisecond to answer his own question. He glanced at Chlothilde, who seemed to know where he was going and nodded imperceptibly for him to stop.

He returned his attention to Diop. "When will the diamonds be ready to be taken to Kadenda?"

"The day after tomorrow. Come back here about eleven. I will have everything ready."

It was a quiet ride back to the hotel. Scary as the previous adventure had been, this one seemed even hairier. Things that glowed in the dark to Ghaddafi over Mobutu and the CIA's dead bodies. What could possibly go wrong?

Martin leaned closer to Chlothilde. "Have you heard from our friend as to when he's going to show up?"

"No, but you know him. He will show up out of the blue and scare us." She smiled. "What else is new with him?"

"Soon would be good. Things are moving fast. We need the whole picture."

She took his hand in hers. "I am as anxious as you. You know him, though. It will be when he is ready, not us."

"Do you have plans for tonight?"

"Yes, and so do you."

"Really?"

"Dinner *chez moi*. My father is coming."

"Hmm . . . Sounds interesting. What have you told him about your favorite mzungu?"

"As little as possible, which is all I know. I did tell him the major was very fond of you, which is more than enough."

"Is he going to know about the real me like everyone else in Kinshasa seems to?"

"Hard to say. He is, of course, well connected, and certainly your former associate Aka was known in many circles. We shall see. Have Hippolyte bring you to my house at seven."

• • •

Martin presented himself at the proper hour appropriately suited and booted, as the major would have put it.

Chlothilde's father was a distinguished, casually-but-expensively dressed older gentleman. That said, Martin found it hard to pin down older Africans' ages. The standard anything from fifty to seventy applied.

He greeted Martin warmly. "Henri Dupasse. Mr. Baker, nice to meet you. Any friend of the major's is a friend of mine." A slight smile played around his lips as he shook Martin's hand.

Martin understood immediately that he knew the whole deal. "I'd love to hear your story. Chlothilde mentioned that the major played a significant role in your life as he did in mine."

"Yes, I heard a little about the Affair Aka, but I did not realize that you were the mzungu involved until Chlothilde mentioned that you knew him and the major. Then I put two and two together."

"Ah, well, it didn't end well for most of us."

"You're alive, which is no small thing, given all of the people who were after you. It is funny, but the circumstances under which I met the major were not entirely dissimilar. Let's discuss it over dinner." He traded glances with Chlothilde. "My daughter is giving me dirty looks."

She clucked affectionately. "Papa, our guest is hungry as well as curious."

Henri ushered them into a magnificent mahogany-paneled room. Zebra skins covered the floors, while antique swathes of bark cloth hung from the walls. All had been put together with the taste of an aesthete, not a showoff.

Over dinner, Henri recounted the whole tale. He'd been a young, idealistic supporter of the Katanganese secession and had ended up a close aide to Tshombe himself. He'd been wounded in a firefight around Elizabethville, and the major, acting then as an unofficial advisor to the UMHK/Tshombe alliance, had saved him. Funny how things never changed. The Anglo-Belgian mining interests were still messing with politics forty-plus years later.

The major, never one to pass up an opportunity for some "intentional networking," had gotten Henri a good job with the mining company and watched him work his way up. Now it was presumably harvest time.

"So where do you and Chlothilde fit into this appropriately murky picture?"

Henri glanced at Chlothilde, who nodded for him to proceed. "While I did not know Aka, it will not surprise you to know that I shared some of his sympathies."

"No surprise there." Martin nodded sympathetically. "But how does that parse with the present?"

"Because I was an investor in Aka's enterprises. Extremely cautiously, of course. My current employer would not understand.

However, old dreams die hard. I presume your interest is entirely personal."

"Not entirely, but significantly. Still, only in Africa could one pile of diamonds weave such a complicated web of competing interests. Two separate guerilla movements, two major intelligence services, and of course Amin's thugs. You're right, though: I want Russell."

"As does our friend."

"Bien sur, for reasons he has not disclosed—at least not to me."

"I believe in his case that they are not related to the past."

"Could certainly be. The major is too much of a pro to take things personally—unless, of course, it threatens his employer's interests. Kadenda did mention Libya as a potential destination, after all. Can't think of anything anyone on our side of things would want shipped there."

"Certainement. Even more so if what we think is headed there is in fact going."

"Things that glow in the dark can certainly attract much attention. At this point, it would seem that all of our interests apart from Russell's are nicely aligned."

Henri rose and waved them out toward the verandah. "Sadly, that may be the only clear thing about this situation. I don't mind telling you that this could—or more likely *is*—going to get extremely dangerous for all of us."

"Which begs the obvious question: what's in this for you and Chlothilde?"

Chlothilde stretched and yawned. "My father's interests are closely aligned with Mobutu's on this. For me, it is perhaps not so clear. However, in my own way, I owe much to the major, but that is a tale for another time."

Martin rose from his chair. "Time for bed. Thank you for an interesting evening. There is one detail we have to sort: the merchandise for Kadenda."

Chlothilde took Martin's arm. "You can give me a ride home. It's on the way to the hotel, and we will go over those details."

* * *

"Is there any reason you didn't want to discuss the merchandise in front of your father?" Martin asked as they left the villa. "Surely he is either providing them or arranging for them to be provided."

"All will be revealed over a nightcap, chez moi."

It was a quiet ride over to Chlothilde's. They both had plenty to think about. Martin was beginning to let in how convolutedly African it was all becoming. Adrenalin, his old best friend and worst enemy, was rearing its ugly head.

"Come in," said the spider to the fly.

Martin sent Hippolyte home, and they stepped inside Chlothilde's place.

She poured each of them a generous snifter of cognac. "Truth or dare time, cher ami. Let's take off our clothes, go to bed, and fill in the blanks."

"Who's first?"

"You, of course. Where are your manners? A gentleman always takes the lead. Eh bien, the major told me a little about the Affair Aka. This Mapende woman must have been pretty special."

"She was to me, and her dream became my dream—always a dangerous thing. Not that I knew it at the time."

"And Agent Russell killed her."

"He didn't pull the trigger himself, but he might as well have."

"Well, Martin, it is a sad fact of life that the Russells of this world rarely pull the trigger."

"True, but I intend to make him pay the bill if I can. Okay, so that's my stuff. And yours? What did the major do for you? He saved my ass and mentored me in his own very offhanded Brit way."

"*Mon histoire* is similar in nature, though the details differ somewhat. As you know, there has been a separatist movement in Shaba almost continuously since independence. You also know where my family's true sympathies lie."

"Like father, like—"

"Yes, and a while back I fell very in love with one of the movement's leaders. I was sneaking out to meet him one night out in the bush near Lubumbashi. It was a trap. One of Surete's agents was waiting to arrest him."

"And?"

"The major had gotten wind of things. Don't ask how. He shot the agent and helped us escape."

"No shit. He's a piece of work, and I bet I don't know the half of it."

"No one does. Even my father does not know about this. He would have killed me for taking such a risk and endangering our family. He would have been right, of course, but I was young."

"Kind of like me. The good news is we're both still young. The better news is that the major has kind of adopted us. The bad news—not that I mind because I owe him more than I can ever repay—is that we now have to stick our necks for him."

"Of course. I love him like the special uncle I never had."

"Or something like that. Speaking of which, you haven't heard from him, have you?"

"Nothing, but I am sure he will appear when we need him. His timing is impeccable. Now enough talk . . ."

10

THE DESK CLERK flagged Martin on his way through the lobby to breakfast and handed him an envelope. Martin loved the young man's Zaïrois uniform: brightly colored pantaloons, embroidered vest, and topped with a distinctly Moroccan-looking fez. He pocketed the envelope and headed through the increasingly crowded lobby toward the dining room.

Even though the fight was still weeks away, the energy was changing, Martin could feel it.

"Mind if I join you?"

It wasn't a question, and worse, it was Russell.

Martin shrugged. "As if I have a choice."

"You don't. Sometimes life just sucks."

"Well, I'm not planning on dying anytime soon, to finish the thought for you."

"There's a decent chance of that if you're a good boy."

The captain seated them at what was becoming Martin's regular table.

Martin always chose a table on the back wall next to the kitchen entrance so he could scan the room for trouble and avail himself of an escape route if needed. One of the first things he did when checking into a new hotel was to map out all the potential escape routes. The major had trained him well.

As soon as the captain was out of earshot, Martin resumed the conversation. "What does that look like?"

"Pretty simple, really. You just have to arrange that piece of transport we discussed last time. Should be easy for a man of your many talents."

"Well, I'm working on a preferred route. Should have things sussed out by the end of the week. I don't suppose you're going to give me any useful info at this point."

"We're not there yet," Russell said with a shake of the head.

"Okay, I'll hang tight."

Russell took himself off, and Martin finally got to the envelope. It was brief and to the point:

Stop by my office at four. Your package will be ready.
— Diop

• • •

Martin noticed a couple of goon types posted at the door when he arrived at Diop's office.

Diop was ready and waiting and handed him a package about the size of a normal first-class envelope.

It no longer surprised Martin how much value could be put in such a small package. Diamonds were a smuggler's, crook's, and spy's best friend. "How much?"

"Not really your business, my friend, but roughly two million US."

"I'll make sure I don't get mugged on the way over to Kadenda's."

"That's very sensible thinking. I can think of at least four sets of people who would be very disappointed if you did, and none of them are the forgiving type."

...

If Hippolyte had any idea what Martin was carrying, he didn't show it as they fought the traffic over to Kadenda's.

Kadenda had his game face on and was all business as he greeted Martin. "This is Monsieur Mlongo. He will check the quality of the consignment."

Mlongo, a tall, cadaverous-looking specimen, nodded brusquely. With the bedside manner of an undertaker, he opened the envelope and poured the stones onto a black velvet cloth that had been laid out on Kadenda's desk. After placing a loupe in his eye, he used tweezers to select a random sampling of the stones. He quickly studied each of them.

Martin watched his face closely for reactions but saw none.

Finished, Mlongo slid the envelope back to Kadenda. "*Ca va.*"

Kadenda waited until Mlongo had left the room. "A man of few words, but they were the right ones. The stones are as advertised. As I said before, it will take seven to ten days to get the transfer done. Will you be paying the ten percent in stones or cash?"

"Stones, please."

"Good. You mentioned there may be some future business."

Martin did his best to respond in a casual tone. "Yeah, assuming this goes well, there's the possibility of another shipment. But it won't be stones. It will be somewhat larger and require special handling."

"Yes, you hinted at that before. We can handle whatever you need." Kadenda rose and offered his hand as he escorted Martin to the door. "I will notify you when the delivery is complete, but I am sure that your people will let you know too."

Game on, Martin thought as Hippolyte drove them back to the Intercontinental. Part One had been pretty smooth. Part Two was going to be much more complicated.

CHAPTER

11

THE NEXT WEEK was quiet. Martin entertained himself by exploring Kinshasa and taking the ferry over to Brazzaville, which was altogether different than its close neighbor across the river. It had an almost somnolent feel compared to Kinshasha's incessant buzz. Chlothilde accompanied him on a few of the outings, but mostly he was on his own. The vibe in town was heating up, though, as the fight drew closer. Foreman and Ali were holding open workouts for the press and assorted hangers-on. It was a circus, but as the major had predicted, the atmosphere provided excellent cover. No one—at least as far as Martin could tell—was interested in the odd mzungu moving around town.

Martin was contemplating attending an open workout Ali had scheduled when Chlothilde bustled into the dining room.

She radiated nervous energy.

"Good morning," he said. "You look like you have news."

"I do. The major got in touch."

"Not before time. I'm all ears. What news?" Martin didn't bother to ask how the major had communicated. She wouldn't have told him anyway.

"He said to pay attention. There will be developments this week."

"That's suitably vague, even by his standards."

"He said that once this thing happens, all will be clear."

"Okay, well, we're in limbo here. Not much happening until we get word back from our friends up north."

"Yes, well, what I really came to tell you is that my father wants us to come to dinner tonight. Someone very important will be there."

"Who?"

"He didn't say, just to be at his place by seven."

Martin raised an eyebrow. "Suitably mysterious that. Formal or informal?"

"Somewhere in the middle," Chlothilde answered as she caressed Martin's hand, "but be prepared to meet some interesting people."

• • •

Martin dressed up as much as comfort would permit, and Hippolyte dropped him at Mr. Dupasse's home promptly at seven. Martin spotted a lot of security around the villa. There was no effort at subtlety, but that wasn't the big man's style. Martin suddenly felt nervous, just as he had while heading toward a planned—or more often *unplanned*—meeting with Amin. Anything could happen in the next few minutes, he told himself. But hopefully he wouldn't have to watch a dictator eat a tortured prisoner's liver. Amin's barbarity still haunted him.

Chlothilde greeted him in the foyer. "Good evening, Baker. Come with me. There are some interesting people here tonight."

It was game time. Chlothilde's use of Martin's assumed name told him everything he needed to know. *On guard, big boy.*

She ushered him out to the veranda, where about a dozen people were gathered. And there he was: Mobutu Sese Seko himself, large as life, wearing his trademark leopard-skin cap.

Chlothilde walked Martin directly to him. "Cher Oncle, may I introduce Trent Baker from America."

Mobutu wasn't big in a physical sense, but he oozed that mixture of cunning and ruthlessness that all big men had and used effectively. He shook Martin's hand firmly while his eyes seemed to X-ray him.

Martin felt naked and vulnerable.

"And so, Mr. Baker, are you here for this little event that I arranged, this so-called Rumble in the Jungle?" Mobutu uttered the last phrase with the faintest of distaste.

"No, your excellency, I'm a businessman looking for opportunities. I'm intrigued by Zairification and *L'authenticite*."

"Very good, mon ami. Someone has taught you the right things to say."

"Or I've done my homework."

Mobutu fell silent—long enough to make Martin wonder if he had ventured too far. Then the president gave a belly laugh and slapped him on the back. "Eh bien, an American with a sense of humor and a penchant for risk. I like it. It makes a pleasant change from those oh-so-serious government types always looking for—how do you say it?—reds under the bed. It's all rather tedious, but they do pay well."

"Monsieur le president, it's indeed an honor to meet you, and I can assure you that I'm neither boring nor on the government payroll."

"So Henri says, and he's usually right." With that, Mobutu moved on and started working the room. The prototypical big man, completely comfortable on what passed for his home turf.

Martin wondered about the size of his payroll, which was rumored to be in the thousands and growing all the time.

"Well, you seem to have made quite the impression." Chlothilde surprised Martin by slipping her arm through his and leading him toward the dining room.

"Aw shucks. I just went with the flow and figured he was probably pretty bored with all of the ass-kissing."

"Be careful. He can be volatile."

"And used to getting his own way from a posse of sycophants. Still, he's altogether a different kettle of fish than Amin."

"Yes, in some ways. Amin is crude, a primal animal, devouring everything in his path. Mobutu is infinitely more subtle, weaves a bigger web. But they both have one thing in common: a penchant for ruthless violence."

"Noted. I plan to stay on his right side—if he has one."

"That can change quickly. Be careful."

"Always."

There was a commotion at the door.

Martin turned to sneak a glimpse and spotted Agent Russell barging in as if he owned the place. "You never know what's going to happen. This is Africa. Speaking of which, look what the cat just dragged in: one of those boring Yank types Mobutu is so fond of. Was he on the guest list?"

Chlothilde grimaced. "Probably. As you said, it's Africa. A man who doesn't keep his bread buttered on both sides soon goes hungry. He gives me the chills every time I see him."

"Well, at least the dinner conversation figures to be interesting. I can't wait."

Russell nodded at Martin and gave Chlothilde a half bow, which might or might not have been piss-taking, as he hustled past them to catch up with Mobutu.

"I really don't like that man," she whispered.

"I neither like him nor trust him. He's the kind of man who goes in the revolving door behind you and comes out in front of you." Martin ushered her into the dining room.

The table was set for ten. No place to hide, Martin thought to himself. Probably a good time to be a brass monkey. As the major always reminded him, listening usually got someone a lot further than talking.

Henri tapped his glass. "Welcome, Monsieur le President. It is an honor to have you in our house and at our table."

"Henri, as always, a pleasure, and what an interesting table you have laid on. You always manage to provide some entertaining new faces." Mobutu nodded toward Martin. "As well as some necessary ones."

The remark seemed to have been directed at the table in general, but Martin noticed Russell fidget slightly with his ear. A tell—another thing the major always taught him to look for. *Duly noted.*

Mobutu eyed Martin. "So, Monsieur Baker, you said you are here on business opportunities. Surely you have favorite in the fight, nevertheless."

Martin took a calming breath before replying. "As it happens, no, Mr. President, but one can't help but get caught up in the general excitement. It's a great showcase for Zaire and yourself, if I might be so bold."

"Yes, it certainly has attracted a lot of attention to us." Like all big men, Mobutu was not immune to flattery, even the most obvious.

Russell offered a plastic smile as he joined the conversation. "Do you have a prediction, Mr. President?"

"Mais non, I have no favorite, at least not that I am admitting to in public," Mobutu replied, making it clear that he did. "The whole event certainly speaks to the strong ties between our countries, doesn't it, Agent Russell?"

"Most certainly, though I've noticed a larger Soviet presence recently."

"Well, they of course remain interested, but I do not presently think you and your patrons should have any cause for concern as long as you remain generous in your support. One must always remember that one cannot buy an African country, as in the bad old days, only rent one."

Russell was like a dog with a bone. "One does always worry that they could be intent on stirring things up in Shaba again."

Martin, stunned, tried to hide the look of disbelief on his face. The CIA agent was either tone deaf, stupid, or arrogant—or all three.

"Well, Agent Russell," Mobutu replied in an icy voice, "I certainly consider seeing that they don't a cost of doing business for you all."

Henri cleared his throat. "Perhaps a subject best left for another time and place."

"Absolutely, Henri. Sometimes our Amis friends can be a little too direct." Mobutu's tone made it very clear that the subject was closed.

The rest of the dinner was spent in more ordinary conversation, much to Martin's—but probably not Russell's—relief. After dessert and digestifs, Russell was the first to depart.

"Bien joue. Well played, Henri," Martin said as he thanked his host afterward. "I can't believe what I just heard."

"Monsieur Russell is neither subtle nor wise, clever though he may think himself to be."

"Let's hope he keeps charging ahead, oblivious to all."

"I have absolutely no doubt he will."

Martin noticed Chlothilde frowning impatiently in the foyer.

Henri seemed to take note as well. "Now I see Chlothilde looking unhappy over there. Goodnight, Monsieur Baker."

"Thank you again," Martin said with a bow.

Chlothilde grabbed Martin's arm and angled them for the

door. "Fortunately, you are a little more subtle than that fellow. What an ugly American."

"And dangerous in spite of it all. Your place or mine."

"*Mechant.*"

"Well, at least I asked. Let's hurry. I don't want to miss the president ascending into the heavens at the nightly sign off." It was one of Martin's favorite pieces of Big Man Schtick. Every night at midnight when Zaire TV signed off, the station played the national anthem against a backdrop of Mobutu ascending into the heavens.

• • •

A few minutes later, they were back at the hotel and suffused in the blue-gray glow from the TV as they snuggled on Martin's bed.

"He was in fine form this evening," Chlothilde said of the president. "He is loving the publicity from the fight."

"It's not easy to compete with Don King, even if you're the president."

"Yes, he is truly an extraordinary person. Quite similar in many ways in that both are the ultimate survivors, but I don't think Mr. King is nearly as dangerous as Mobutu."

"Agreed. Nor does he have the president's sense of timing." Martin gestured toward the screen while Mobutu made his nightly ascension. "King would kill for that."

12

MARTIN ROSE EARLY the next morning and finished breakfast before the fight hordes swamped the dining room. He decided to take a stroll to clear the cobwebs, but just as he exited the hotel, a dusty Land Rover pulled up beneath the awning, Agent Russell behind the driver's wheel.

"Hop in. We're going for a spin." It wasn't a question.

Martin climbed in. "That was some show you put on at dinner last night."

"Never pays to let a client get too comfortable."

"He didn't seem very impressed with you. Personally, I'm not so sure the Moscow folks are so pushy, but you should know better than I if you can get away with that heavy-handed shit. I don't need to remind you that this is Africa. Things can change fast."

Russell rolled his eyes. "Okay. Are you finished with your little sermon? We're going to take a little drive."

• • •

Russell's little drive turned out to be a ninety-plus-minute excursion into the bush. They left the paved roads early, which wasn't hard to do in Zaire, and the rutted murram roads deteriorated rapidly. Conversation was sparse.

Martin took in the scenery. He was pretty sure this was what being inside of a cement shaker felt like. As he bounced and jounced on the hot metal passenger's seat, he made a mental note: Rovers were practical, perhaps, but not built for comfort.

After an excruciating thirty minutes, the road disappeared completely, and they headed cross country. Zaire had countless climate zones. Kinshasa was carved out of rain forest. The area to the south was drier—not quite high savannah, but a long way from tropical jungle.

"Nice and private," Martin mused aloud. "If you're bringing me out here to shoot me, you could have done that easily enough twenty minutes or half an hour ago."

"Or at least five other times since you landed. Luckily for you, I have use for your talents, as you shall soon see."

They pulled up to a shack that was obviously functioning as a guard post. A couple of kali-wielding types sidled out far enough to recognize Russell and wave them through. They didn't look official. Neither did the base, encampment, or whatever else Martin wanted to call the collection of ramshackle huts and lean-tos that dotted the clearing.

"Gee, Steve, this doesn't look like your guys' usual style to me."

Russell didn't comment but parked the Rover under a shade tree next to the only solid structure: a cinderblock-on-cement building with a roofed verandah. The three guards manning the perimeter looked more awake than their counterparts at the gate. Inside, three unshaven, armed mzungus sat around a rickety table, nursing beers.

"Ami, who is this mzungu?" The largest started to rise, sliding his hand casually but purposefully toward his holster.

Martin couldn't place the accent. Hispanic of some kind.

The speaker relaxed as Russell waved him down.

"Someone we may well need later. Trent Baker, meet Raoul, Jose, and Jesus."

Fuck me, Martin thought. There probably wasn't a real name involved. It was like a bad B movie, except they all looked the part: mean-snake dangerous.

He nodded. They didn't look like they'd be easily impressed. Less was more.

"He's young, gringo."

"Trust me. He can handle himself. I know from personal experience."

Temporarily mollified, the leader lumbered over to a cooler and handed each of them a beer.

The beer was an elixir for Martin's parched throat. He killed half of it.

"Bueno," the leader said, "where are we with the plan? This is not an exciting place."

Russell took a swig and wiped his mouth clean. "Things will happen soon. I'm awaiting confirmation of the date of the next shipment, which I believe will be on the same day as the fight. Everyone will be focused on security for the event, especially the Surete. Just think who's going to be there. Perfect time to move sensitive materials on the other side of town from 20 May Stadium."

"Bueno, all good," the leader said with a skeptical frown, "except we have to have absolutely accurate information."

"I will have that. As you know, we track all shipments very carefully."

"Si, and will there be any Ami guards?"

"Doubt it, but won't know until closer to the date."

Once more, the leader didn't look satisfied. "Okay. Then what?"

Russell nodded to Martin. "That's where Baker comes in. He's good at exporting sensitive materials."

"Has he moved this type of material before?"

"Have you all stolen it before?" Russell shot back.

Now if I could only figure out what they're talking about, Martin thought. He didn't dare ask, but things were beginning to add up in a bad way. No wonder the major was interested.

"No," the leader finally answered, "but why do we need this other gringo?"

"Because he's American and will look like he works for us—something none of you could be accused of. Besides, folks with Cuban accents are frowned on around here, in case you hadn't noticed."

"Si, senor." The insolence dripped from the words hanging in the air.

Martin wondered how Russell would react. His skin was parchment-thin.

"Listen, Amigo. I know where you live. Remember that. One more word from you and you won't like your new accommodation. "

That killed the conversation for a bit, and everyone sipped at their beers in a tenuous silence. Martin wondered who would break first.

It was Russell. "Okay, folks. That wasn't a very good way to start, so why don't we just start over? This is Trent Baker. He will take the cargo and expedite it over the border once you've obtained it."

Martin ventured his first question. "May I ask how bulky this cargo will be?"

"Three wooden crates," Russell answered. "Small but heavy."

"Can I carry them in one vehicle?"

"Yes, but more on that later. The important thing is that you all know and recognize each other. I'll be there most likely, but just in case."

Martin wanted to know more. "And?"

"These fine gentlemen will leave somewhat wealthier for their services, and you and I will continue on."

The leader drained the last of his beer and tossed it onto the ground. "And when will this happen?"

"When else? The night of the fight." Russell smiled. "Every Surete, police, and military man will be guarding the big event. We'll be on the other side of town, where things will be relatively quiet."

"You seem mighty sure of yourself," Martin said.

"Should be. I drew up the security plans personally."

Martin did the calendar math: twelve days and counting. Things were getting close, and he still had no real idea what was going on. Where the hell was the major? One thing was for sure: he didn't trust Russell as far as he could throw him, and he doubted the Cubans did either.

Russell stood up and shook the Cubans' hands. "We're done here. You all have met, and you will get your instructions closer to the date."

The Cubans didn't offer to shake, which didn't offend Martin. *Fuck it*, he thought. They were all cannon fodder as far as Russell was concerned. Things were about to get interesting, and the Cubans looked like they had been there and done that. *Memo to the major.*

"Let's go, Sunshine." Russell started for the Rover.

Martin followed him and climbed in for the bone-jarring ride back to Kinshasa.

"How'd you like the compadres?" Russell asked as soon as they were on their way.

"They looked mean enough. I'm assuming you know what you're dealing with. Not sure I'd want to piss them off."

"If all goes well, you won't have to."

"Why does that not inspire confidence? Now that we're getting closer, do you want to tell me exactly what's going on? I mean, this is clearly off the books."

"True enough. Like I said before, a man gets to my age, he starts thinking about a pension."

"Jesus, Russell, that's fucking rich."

"That's exactly what I'm *not* right now."

"So we're going to divert a shipment that glows in the dark up north to the Mad Colonel, and poof—your worries melt away."

"You put things together pretty quick."

Yeah, Martin thought to himself. *Maybe quicker than you think.* He could see everything unfolding in Russell's warped brain. Martin would be the perfect stooge. Russell would let him complete the job, making sure to be one step behind the whole way, and then have the colonel dispose of the inconvenient link while he pocketed his pension and looked like a hero for having tried to stop things.

"What's in it for me?"

"Maybe not quite a Park Avenue pension, but enough to go eat burgers on the desert island of your choice for the rest of this go-round."

Martin could have and should have been offended, but he knew it was best to keep Russell thinking he was a stoned-out piece of cannon fodder. The man was a walking cliché, the prototypical ugly American—and an arrogant one to boot. *You can't make this up*, Martin thought, and yet there was Russell, sitting next to him with a shit-eating grin on his face. Large as life and mamba-mean.

"Probably better than Tripoli."

"I'm sure I'll think of something besides that."

They lapsed into their own thoughts for the rest of the tedious ride back to town.

Martin turned everything over in his head. There had to be some way out of here, said the joker to the thief, but he needed the major's devious mind to answer Dylan's riddle.

• • •

The clerk handed Martin a note with his key. The scent said the note was from Chlothilde, but it reminded him of Esther again, and he melted a little inside.

Chez moi, huit heures.

Dinner at eight. Don't be late. He'd have a tale to tell for sure.

• • •

Chlothilde met him at the front door. "Eh bien, monsieur, do I have a surprise for you." She stepped aside, and there, standing beside Henri, was the major about as close to beaming as Martin could remember seeing him.

"Bloody good to see you, old cock."

Martin felt a surge of relief. "Likewise, and not before time. Things are getting interesting fast, and I for one need your devious brain."

"Well, in you come, and we can get to it after dinner."

They kept it light and old-timey over the meal—wise because of the staff—but Martin was bursting with questions.

Afterward, the major gave Chlothilde a lopsided smile. "How about a snifter of your excellent cognac and a fine Havana by your charming pool."

"Major, *tu es mechant.* We are all anxious for that." She grasped his arm and steered him out to the pool.

"Mechant mais pas sot."

Naughty but not stupid—understatement of the decade, Martin thought. He lit and puffed on the excellent Punch cigar the butler passed around. He should have been surprised but somehow wasn't when Chlothilde took a cigar and lit it like a pro.

She gave the major an impish grin. "Just another of the bad habits you taught me."

"To which you took like a duck to water."

"So," Martin said, "where to start? Our old friend Russell is very much around. Today he took me on an interesting drive to meet some less-than-salubrious Cuban types."

"Hmm . . . No surprise that. Our boy really has gone all in on going off the reservation. That's not all; he's fitting you up nicely."

"That thought did dawn on my sometimes-slow brain today. It ran something like this. I take the goods to Tripoli, get killed by his buddies, and he claims the Cubans and I did it, that he tried valiantly and failed to stop it. Then he collects the payoff and lives to scam another day. Not all that subtle—but effective."

"Well, he's not a subtle chap. His sort isn't. But they can be dangerous enough in their blundering way."

"Mon Ami." Henri circled the table with the cognac. "This is so you. None of us have more than a small piece of this histoire. Well, we are all here. There is plenty of this excellent cognac left, and the cigars are burning nicely."

"Yes, when you put it like that." The major puffed a bit and gathered his thoughts. "This all actually, in a funny way, goes back to Uganda."

Everything seemed to go back to Uganda, Martin thought ruefully. "I'll never escape that place."

"Perhaps not, friend, but here's your chance to pass some of that pain back to the psychopath who thoroughly deserves it, who not only caused your pain but is looking to get you killed to finish the tale."

Chlothilde shuddered. "We need a strong Nganga for that man. He terrifies me."

The major nodded his approval. "As he should, my dear. Some of the things he has been party to with Amin over the last two years do not bear repeating in any company."

"There have been horrible tales," Henri said, "even to our somewhat jaded ears."

"You don't know the half of it," the major replied. "Oddly enough, he really seemed to go off the beam—completely, I mean—after the Affair Aka. Before that there were various folks in his inner circle who had some degree of input. Now our man Russell and "Bullet Bob" Astles are calling the tune."

"Astles . . . I have heard that name." Henri appeared to search his memory. "Ah, yes, the cashiered sergeant major from the King's African Rifles when Amin served in them."

"Yes, he was booted for stealing the mess funds. He has surpassed that with Amin. He's called Bullet Bob because he persuaded Amin that using bullets on all of his opponents that he was slaughtering was too expensive."

Henri frowned. "Not sure I like where this is going."

"You won't. His solution was to have the prisoners line up single file and give the one at the end a hammer to start crushing the skulls of the ones in front of them. When their arms gave out, the next one took over. The last one standing got to start the next day. Hence the dark humor of Bullet Bob."

"That story never gets better, no matter how many times I hear it." Martin took a big swig of the cognac. "I know he'd like a piece of me."

"Quite right, old chap. You earned it. Near as I can figure, they got friendly aborting your and Aka's operation. The next piece of the equation was when Amin started flirting with the Libyans after he went off the Israelis."

"I'd left by then."

"Good thing too. He disposed your protector about two weeks after you left."

"Bulyanezi? I get it. He was the Israeli's blue-eyed boy. No pun intended. How'd you skate, Major? We were seen a lot around town together."

"Oh, I spun a yarn that I knew you were up to something and was trying to find out. Plus, with the aid of certain friends here, I gave them parts of Aka's network that had already been compromised, not that Astles, Amin, and crew knew at the time. They were jolly grateful too."

"Ah hah. Now I get why Russell let me go. I owe you more than I thought, and I already owed you a lot." Martin raised his snifter and drained it. "Am I the last person here to know all this?"

"All of what, old boy? We're only at the end of the beginning."

"I was afraid of that, and it's past time to—"

"Quite, and I'm getting to it, be assured. It seems that our man Russell saw the light—or should I say darkness?—when he had to hand over your diamonds to Mobutu's folks after your old friend Bullet Bob took his and Amin's cut."

"Yeah, he played the old 'I ain't got no pension blues' to me too."

"Can't say the thought doesn't occur from time to time, but certainly not in the way he has chosen to do it. Plenty of loose change around, so to speak, without empowering the likes of Gaddafi."

Henri refreshed everyone's cognacs. "We may need these. This whole affair is turning quite horrifying. Am I correct in assuming that Monsieur Gaddafi will not be trifling with diamonds?"

The major stared into his drink. "No prizes for stating the

obvious. He wants cobalt and uranium. No additional prizes for guessing for what purpose."

"Probably worth a lot more than diamonds," Martin said.

"Yes, and more importantly, after Russell has fitted you up for the job, Gaddafi will give Russell the way to spend his pension."

Martin grimaced. "Well, thanks for putting me in the hot seat."

"Yes, well, I may have put you there, but I bloody well don't plan to leave you sitting there."

"So please do enlighten us."

"A simple variation on the shell game will do."

Martin liked the sound of that. Mostly. "Simple, but not necessarily easy. Agreed."

"Remember, old boy, we do have one distinct advantage: Russell himself won't be with you."

"But watching carefully, I'm sure. Plus there's the little matter of me getting disposed of by Gaddafi's boys, even if we hadn't done the switch."

"Granted, an equation in several variables, but all very solvable. First, I must do some serious recce as to the facts on the ground, and then, of course, we have to inform our good friends here."

"So," Martin said, "I presume you're sticking around for the duration."

"Of course. The fun is just beginning. I've rented a little pied a terre in a more discreet part of town, or should I say that our local partners have?"

"And they would be?"

"Our friends from New York and other related types. The good news is that you're playing on the right side of the blanket this time."

"Hope so. Trusting you on that one. Still, this is getting complicated."

"Quite, old chap, and we're just getting started, but shame on us if we can't bait and switch a bull in the China shop like Russell."

Henri passed the cognac around once more. "Monsieur Russell had already worn out his welcome before the contretemps at dinner the other night. It's now personal for Mobutu. That can't be a good thing for Russell."

"Or us, if he moves too fast." The major relit his cigar and puffed meditatively. "As you all know, there are a lot of moving pieces here. Much to sort out. We're going to have to have an overall plan but one that can flex, because for sure things won't play out like we think they will. Never do."

"Bien sur," Henri said, "the voice of experience, as I recall. I am sitting here as a result of one such deviation."

"Me too," Martin said.

The major almost looked like he was blushing. "We've been summoned to a meeting tomorrow morning, Martin. Details to follow, but Hippolyte will know before you do."

Martin laughed. "You old fox. I knew he was a plant."

13

HIPPOLYTE WAS WAITING outside the hotel at nine o'clock sharp the next morning.

"Where we headed?" Martin asked.

Hippolyte, leaning against his dusty, beat-up Peugeot, offered a nonchalant smile. "You will see."

"Fine," Martin said. "It's not like I know Kinshasa well enough to recognize any placenames."

One thing was for sure: they weren't headed to the expensive expat part of town. After about a thirty-minute ride through increasingly poor areas of town, they slowed to a stop in front of a mean-looking brick building with a peeling mustard-yellow façade.

Martin entered through the front door. He should have been but somehow wasn't surprised to see the major and Etienne Tshishkedi seated at a decrepit table. "Well, well. Quel surprise, as in not. Not up to your usual standard's, Etienne."

"Nice to see you again too." Etienne, dressed in the usual tailored suit, smiled and waved him to a feeble-looking wood chair that looked like it would barely accommodate his weight. "Our business requires a low profile at the moment."

"This certainly fits that bill, though I must say you're quite overdressed for this part of town. Is this the part where I get some clue what's actually going on?"

The major smiled. "This is the part where you get to know as much as we do. Unfortunately, that's not everything by a fair bit."

"Can't wait. Let's have it. While we're at it, I assume that you've told Etienne that our good friend Russell already has me fitted up."

"Certainement," Etienne said. "He wants no witnesses, and you were expendable from Lamu on."

"Actually, a good bit before that, but who's counting?" The major smiled, warming to his task. He so obviously loved the stuff. "This all gets a bit complicated, so bear with me." He beamed. "Mr. Russell has made this all a bit complicated. Etienne knows a bit of this, but you don't. You see, it's all fine and good if Russell and crew pull this off, but the real prize would be for them to pull it off without anyone knowing it went to our friend Gaddafi."

"Yeah, sure, and Mobutu's not going to scream bloody murder when a shipment—"

"Of course, but that's where your Cuban amigos come in."

"I thought they were cheap, independent muscle."

"All of that, but cheap muscle normally associated with our friends in Moscow."

Martin thought through the details. "So they do the hijack, he quietly kills them, then has me smuggle it up to Benghazi, has me offed, and everyone assumes it ended up in Moscow."

"Actually, Sarov, old boy. That's where the Russkis assemble the bombs. Otherwise, that's not a bad start at connecting the dots."

"Jeez, that almost smacks of your type of thinking, Major."

"Even the proverbial blind pig. Yes, it's not all bad. However, putting a spike in it will be as simple as the mechanics of it, methinks."

"Bien sur, mon ami," Etienne said with a flourish. "We will simply ambush the ambushers."

The major drew back as a sour look appeared on his face. "Absolutely not, dear chap. That's the last thing we want to do, really."

"Pour quoi?"

"Because if we do it that way, Russell will still be able to deny involvement. We must wait and watch patiently and then turn the whole lot over at the Libyan border. Game, set, and match."

"Should work well enough," Martin said with more confidence than he felt. "Just make sure I don't get lost in translation or win an all-expenses-paid trip to Abu Salim." He turned to Etienne. "I assume we want to keep this close to the vest for the time being."

"Certainement, I have a few trusted men in mind. Besides, as you know, Russell and his people have suborned many in the Surete. They have the money, the motivation, and most of all, the paranoia. Otherwise, I would just out Monsieur Russell and stop the whole thing before it starts."

"I quite see that," the major said. "Still, security is going to have be very tight on this. The obvious question is how we figure out where Russell is going to make his move. That's where you come in, Martin."

Martin frowned. "Why do I always get the plumb jobs?"

"Really, old boy?"

"Knew I shouldn't have said it before it was halfway out. So my question is, who are you and Etienne going to use to hijack Russell's hijackers when this all plays out?"

"I have four extremely reliable men who are loyal only to me," Etienne said. "They are not officially employed by the Surete, so the Amis have not brought them."

"Good by me. If the major trusts you, I do. But it all rests on me not only getting the necessary info on time but being able to deliver it to you all. That might not be so easy if I'm in Russell's back pocket."

The major nodded. "Quite, we'll be keeping a very close eye on you all."

Martin still wasn't satisfied. "No offense, you two—you're the pros here—but how are we going to keep all these spooks from tripping over each other?"

"Well, old boy, this won't be a doddle, but we will handle things. Etienne and I have worked together before, several times, always to good effect."

"Question, Major," Martin said, still sorting through the details. "Russell doesn't already know you're in town, he soon will. How's he going to feel about that?"

"I spun him a bit of a yarn that Mobutu's folks, namely Etienne here, have brought me in to shake the trees a bit in Shaba, given my old connections with the separatists there. That covers all the bases neatly. Besides, he'll have his mind on other things."

Martin leaned forward, propping his elbows on the rickety table. "Well, there's just one other bit to go over before we're done. Major, what's going to be in your hand when it comes out of the cookie jar?"

The major looked almost embarrassed—something Martin thought impossible. "Meaning, what's in it for us? Well, there's one minor detail, really, that sweetens the pot for everybody. We want you to run the goods right up to the border. We want Russell completely incriminated. And we want to roll up the rest of his corrupted network and a few Libyans as a bonus while we're at it."

"Ambitious."

"But sweet revenge on your buddy Russell. Who knows? If things work out really well, we might get him a not-so-private suite at Malaka."

Martin leaned back, satisfied—at least for now. "Next moves, gentlemen?"

"Just keep doing what you're doing for now, old boy."

"I'm going to Shaba for a few days just to look around and to be seen in all the right places by all the wrong people."

"Eh bien, I have a day job," Etienne said with a laugh. "Monsieur Baker, would you like to attend any of the fight festivities? That can certainly be arranged. It wouldn't hurt."

"I'll consider it. I'm lucky in that I have an excellent local guide."

"One who is not only attractive but capable of opening many doors." Etienne smiled. "So, mes amis, I think our business is concluded for today."

Martin turned to the major. "I assume Hippolyte can get you messages."

"Of course. He's very reliable, and you can trust him as you would me."

Martin decided to let that one ride, shook hands all around, and left them to it. Probably best not to hear what they were talking about, anyway. He wasn't exactly thrilled about the proposed scheme. It certainly couldn't be dignified with the word "plan." He knew the major would come up with something better—if they had the time. That was the X factor, for sure.

• • •

Things were jumping back at the hotel. It was another Don King extravaganza full throttle. The human Brillo pad was smoking like a Baptist minister. Sweat stained his pink silk suit as he gesticulated wildly toward the heavens, wiping droplets of sweat off his chin with a handkerchief. The press boys were lapping it up. Nothing trained a man for running a good press event like street-corner-hustle oratory.

Martin stopped to watch for a while. Why not? It was free. The guy was good, even if he was bad to the bone.

Someone grabbed Martin's elbow, and Martin pivoted.

"Tranquilo, senor, your friend wants to see you." It was one of Russell's Cubans.

Just what the day had been missing, Martin thought ruefully. He realized he had no choice but to follow the man out to the waiting vehicle.

Russell smiled as soon as they made eye contact. "Sorry to drag you away. He's good, isn't he?"

"Somehow I'm surprised he's not on your payroll. Or is he?"

"If he is, I ain't saying. Hop in. We're going to take a little drive."

Once again, it wasn't an invitation. Martin suddenly felt naked, which he was. Out on the limb. No cover. The only consolation was that they still needed him.

Not that the fact made him feel any better when they slipped a blindfold over his head.

"Really, Russell, even by your standards—"

"Completely necessary, as you'll see when we get there. By the way, we'll be stopping in a bit to leave off Juan and Pedro. This one will be solo for just you and I."

Martin didn't find the idea entirely reassuring. He was left to his own thoughts as they jolted along an abysmal road for about forty-five minutes. He tried to take in the sounds and smells to get some sense of where they were going, but the blindfold was tight and stunk of stale sweat. The Rover was bucking and heaving, and he was hanging on for dear life—a full-time occupation. *So much for that exercise.*

Mercifully, they lurched to a halt just as Martin began feeling nauseous.

Agent Russell snatched the blindfold, and it took Marin's eyes a few moments to adjust to the overpowering glare of the early afternoon sun. They were in front of a good-sized bunker, surrounded by a tall chain-link fence. The place was crawling with

Zairean troops as well as some heavily armed mzungus, obviously mercenaries, whose eyes constantly scanned the compound. In contrast to the Zairians', the mercenaries' weapons gleamed immaculately, safeties off. The fetid stench of the neighboring jungle made Martin temporarily dizzy.

"Bonjour, mes Amis," a barrel-chested guard said. "I am bringing someone from the embassy to inspect your security."

Someone had to have called ahead. They were waved inside.

Another guard, this one taller but leaner than the last, unlocked a heavy-looking vault like door and clipped badges on their shirts.

"Radiation counters," Russell said. "We don't want you glowing in the dark with your lady friend tonight."

Russell was such an endearing guy. Martin was summoning up something nasty to say when the door swung open on massive hydraulic hinges. Cold air blasted out as they stepped into a vast room lined with shelves stacked with what looked like mini safes.

Martin studied the cargo a moment. "Okay, I know what they are. How many am I expected to move?"

"Six or eight, but we won't know exactly until the night of the diversion. Before you ask, they weigh roughly a hundred pounds apiece. Lead's heavy."

"Yeah, not my normal cargo—that's for sure."

"You're a smart boy. Your partners are probably smarter or at least more experienced. You'll think of something."

Martin ignored Russell's condescension. "How much time do we have to get ready?"

"We're figuring the night of the fight will be perfect. Everyone in Kinshasa that counts will be there. Most importantly, every cop and soldier. We'll jump the shipment the other side of town. Not a ton of time, but we'll figure out something."

"Hopefully something a little more concrete. Speaking of

which, you need to be a little more specific about what I'm getting paid for this little expedition."

"Half a million in the manner of your choice."

"Please. Gaddafi's paying you a lot more than that. Plus, there's the little matter of my continued discretion. Also, of course, I'll have expenses. No way it gets done for less than a cool million. Don't bother. That's not negotiable."

Russell didn't bat an eyelash. "Half down, the rest on successful delivery. The balance will ensure your discretion, plus the fact that a word in the wrong ear and Mobutu and folks will think you did it."

Martin knew the whole exchange was bogus. He had no choice but to play along. Anyway, Russell wouldn't be able to weasel out of putting the half million into a secure bank account of the major's choice.

The jarring drive back to Kinshasa was quiet. Martin had a lot to think about, and he figured Russell did too.

Russell dropped him at the hotel with a cursory nod. "I'll leave you a few days to get things lined up."

CHAPTER

14

As soon as Martin got back to the hotel, he called Chlothilde. Things were ramping up. It was time for some serious scheming, as the major would say.

"Eh bien, Martin, we will have dinner here tonight. I will make sure everyone who needs to be here will be."

When he got there at seven, it was a full house: the major, Tshishkedi, Diop, Henri, and of course, Chlothilde.

"Well, old cock, this is what we signed up for." The major was beaming with the thrill of the hunt.

Martin didn't quite share his excitement, but maybe that was because he was the bait—the goat tethered to the stake. "Well, as they say down on the farm, we're getting to nut-cutting time. Pardon my concern, but it's mine in play, and right now we don't have much of a plan."

"True enough," the major replied, "so let's get down to it. I'm assuming everyone here is in the know. So my first question is to Monsieur Diop. How are we proposing to transfer the goods? I'm assuming by plane."

"Certainement. The question is what landing strip." Diop glanced around expectantly.

"Amongst many others—questions that is, mon ami." Tshishkedi got up and started pacing. "Sorry, but I think better when I am walking. What strip? What equipment? When do we hijack the hijack? To name a few."

The major nodded. "All very relevant, mon ami. However, may I suggest that we start at the beginning? Slow and steady will win this race. So, Etienne, the obvious first question is where Russell and his lads will look to do the hijack."

"That is not so hard," Etienne said. "Did not Monsieur Russell say that they would do it as far from the stadium as possible? I suggest we select the spot by leaking the route in such a way as to limit the possibilities. Vraiment, though the more important point is surely where we will perform the second."

"Has to be at the strip, old boy, but we want to track them from the heist to the airfield to make sure that there's no triple-cross. Russell isn't brilliant, but he *is* devious. I want to cover all contingencies. Our friend Martin would be an excellent red herring if Russell smells a rat."

Henri passed around a humidor. "Etienne, don't you all have something out by Matete?"

"Yes, we haven't used it in a while, but it will suffice, especially if it is just for show. Speaking of which, Diop, I assume you have access to a plane and pilot."

Diop was quick to answer. "Of course. Several. But Kinshasa can sometimes be a small place. Russell may also use them when it suits his purposes."

"That's not altogether a bad thing." The major puffed contentedly. "Punch, if I'm not mistaken. Jolly useful for him to know Martin has made the necessary arrangements."

Martin was growing impatient. "So where do we jump them, and what do we do with the Cubans—and Russell, for that matter?"

"Much as we all would probably like to dispose of them, I think a spell in Makala contemplating their many sins might do all three of them a world of good. What say you, Etienne?"

"Bien sur," Etienne said with a wry smile, "and I am sure that Monsieur le Presidente will extract suitable reparations from the Amis for what will be an extremely embarrassing incident for all involved."

"Quite, and he will be entitled to them. Plus, there will be the small matter of Martin and my reward."

"He can and will be generous, as you know."

"Our assignment is to be around to collect."

Martin got up and stretched. "Personally, as someone who's ass will be primarily on the line, I wish we had a little better handle on things."

"That will be all of our jobs over the next few days. Etienne, Diop, you must mobilize your networks." Henri passed the cognac again. "Their security won't be perfect. It never is. In the meantime, Diop and I will put arrangements in place for the flight out of Matete. I am sure our Amis will hear of it one way or another. Etienne, mon vieux, you must find a discreet way to keep tabs of the Cubans."

"Bien sur," Etienne said, "that can be easily done. We know generally where they are all the time."

The major steered the conversation back to Martin. "Best for you and Monsieur Diop to be quite visible around town the next few days. Maybe a lunch at the Intercontinental, just to keep Russell interested."

Martin mulled over the possibilities. "How about front row seats at the big prefight concert? Le tout Kinshasa will be there. I'm hoping that Henri or Etienne can pull on a few strings and get at least three tickets, because I'd love to take Chlothilde."

"Martin," Chlothilde said with an impish smile, "you are

mechant. You know Papa has to now."

"Not mechant, my dear. Clever. Learns fast, even if he is a Yank." That was about as close as the major was ever going to come to a compliment. "Etienne?"

"Of course, not a problem. Not sure about front row, as my employer will be sitting there with Don King and their entourages."

The major appeared satisfied. "Anywhere within five rows will do, methinks. It's going to be a hell of a show. It's the greatest assemblage of soul and R&B acts ever put together."

Henri rose. "Good. I think that settles things for tonight."

• • •

Chlothilde was quiet on the ride home and loud in bed afterward.

Martin found himself struggling to read her. "Eh bien, cherie. What's with you tonight?"

"I don't know," she said softly, "but it all seemed to get real tonight. I think it is the first time I realized how dangerous this will be."

"That has been dawning on me, but truth be told, I knew it when I got on the plane."

"So why, cher? What's in it for you? Just revenge?"

Martin shook his head. "It's not that simple. It's *never* that simple. Sure, revenge is a biggie. Russell is a worthless scumbag. Then there's the fact that I owe the major."

"That doesn't seem like enough to justify the risks. One thing I am reminded of every day here is that karma and righteous revenge are for books and movies. This is Africa. There are no moral absolutes—never have been."

"The heart of darkness, eh? And I'm Kurtz." Martin chuckled.

"It's not funny, Martin. You were drawn into it. I am not sure you emerged."

I'm not so sure, either—and even less sure it matters."

"But of course it matters, and I hope you have some moral absolutes. Africa no, but you—absolutely necessary."

Martin thought for a moment. "I'd like to think I have them—in theory, of course. My fear is around here they can get you killed. I guess you could say I'm involved in a way around a moral absolute. Russell must pay for his sins."

"That's a little too cynical and easy."

"True, but one of the things I've noticed is that the veneer of civilization is thin hereabouts. You only have to scratch a little to get back to the limbic loop—feeding, fighting, and fucking. Once you get there, it's hard to step back and regain your perspective."

"But you must," she said in a resolute voice, "or you become one of them."

"Too right. The seduction of the dark side, cloaked in survival instinct—potent combination. Maybe a part of me is doing this to break of the spell."

"I hope so, mon cher. Mais, you all seem caught up in it. You, the major, my father— everyone. I don't know. Sometimes I wonder if it is worth it or even makes sense."

"Surely not letting Gaddafi get his hand on nukes makes sense."

"Yes, of course. There is that. The only problem is that you all seem to have other motivations."

"Yeah, well life can be complicated."

"You can do better than that. Are you that wounded, that cynical at your age?"

"Funny, I never thought of it that way."

"Maybe, but I think you have been thinking too much and feeling too little."

She had a point, he thought, as he'd been a thoroughly medicated puddle of self-pity since that day on Lamu. On autopilot, out to lunch. He shook himself like a dog. He felt cold and scared inside. Suddenly, he was really there. He could smell her scent mingled with his own fear-tinged sweat. It was like the film had been ripped off and he could suddenly see and feel clearly and more acutely than he ever had. *Fuck me*, he thought. *Feels like I'm waking up out of a dream into a nightmare.*

"Hey, are you all right?" She hugged him, and he hung on for dear life. "You look even whiter than usual." She caught herself and started laughing.

He joined her, and they broke into deep belly laughs.

The tension drained from him. "How can I be whiter than I already am?"

"But you are, and suddenly you had that little-boy scared look."

"You know I probably should be."

"Why aren't you? You should be. The last time you played with Russell and these types, it didn't end very well for you."

"Hope—or should I say adrenalin?—springs eternal."

"It would be nice if for once you wouldn't be so cynical."

"Necessary survival skill around these parts."

She caressed his cheek. "*Dommage*, you have an answer for everything and a solution for nothing. If you don't agree with me, tell me why you all are playing the same games over and over."

That was an uncomfortable thought. He wasn't sure what to do with it. "Let me get back to you on it."

"Please think, Martin. You are young. My father and the major—and I say this loving them both—have been doing this so long they don't know how to do anything else."

"I can't walk at this point. I'm all in. Other people are counting on me."

"I understand, but hopefully, unlike my father and the major, you won't be playing these dangerous games when you grow up."

"When I grow up . . . I wonder what that will look like."

"Different if you want to get to their age. Let's sleep."

Easier said than done, Martin thought. He lay there thinking about what Chlothilde had said. Answers easy or hard eluded him. *Fuck it and drive on*, he thought. *In for a penny*. He tried to think how the major would answer but couldn't. Definitely a discussion to be had.

Agent Russell interrupted Martin's breakfast the next morning, seating himself once more as if he were an invited guest. "They really do a good breakfast here."

"I can see your fond of it. Food's good, but the company's lousy."

"Come now. Is that any way to talk to your partner?"

"It'd be better if you were an invisible one."

"No such luck. How are your preparations coming?"

"Should be fine. I'll be confirming everything later today. Any changes I need to know about? Still fight night?"

"Absolutely. Can't think of a better cover."

"As long as we're doing it on the other side of town. Same payload?"

"Yep."

"Which brings me to the sticky question of my fee. Shall we take a stroll in the garden and discuss it?" Martin signaled for the bill, and they headed out into the garden.

Once they were strolling alone beside a flower bed of exotic annuals, Martin felt safe to continue. "You do realize that the expenses for this little exercise are going to be on the heavy side. Plus, it's obviously your retirement fund, not that your buddy there won't pay you well for future services rendered. So security, namely mine, is a big driver for me."

Russell winced as though he were embarrassed but couldn't quite pull it off.

"There's another not completely inconsequential matter. Being as how I trust you not in the slightest, how are you going to convince me that you won't kill me and everyone else involved the minute you get the crates—not to mention pay us in a way that can't be traced?"

"The pay part is easy. Swiss or other offshore accounts. The other part is, of course, more difficult, especially since I won't be going to Libya right away."

"I assumed that, but I'm not in the slightest bit inclined to visit our slightly nuts buddy up north. Why can't the Cuban boys do that part of the gig?"

"That was my plan."

"And for the rest? If you're thinking that we just show up with enough guns for mutually assured destruction at the exchange, don't think so. Nope, I'm going to want a smoking gun—something that will hang your miserable ass if you're thinking of another Lamu bait and switch."

Russell nodded. "What's that look like to you?"

"A signed confession. It's got to be something that lasts. What's to prevent you from turning me into Mobutu and his cronies and your spook buddies when this is all done? Or were you fitting up the Cubanos for that one?"

"The thought had occurred."

"You're going to need some cannon fodder, and they would fit the bill nicely. Mind you, Mobutu and friends won't be happy if they have no one to take out their anger on."

"They'll get over it, and there's plenty more uranium here."

"What have you promised the Cubanos?"

"Money, of course, but something far more valuable than that: US citizenship."

"Easy for you. They'll never get out of Libya."

"My guess would be no."

Martin kept pressing. "Don't you think they've thought about that?"

"It may have occurred to them, but they're simple *campesinos*. Besides, they don't get paid until delivery to wherever the mad colonel wants them delivered to."

"So, all that's left is me."

"Yes, but that's not as easy as it sounds, either. I need guarantees also."

Martin had thought of that already. "For sure. So the letter will have to implicate both of us and be signed by both of us."

"And we each have a copy."

"Which leads to a bunch of other questions. Where will we keep them? Shit happens."

"So why don't we sleep on things and talk in a few days? It's still a while to the main event." Russell held out his hand.

"Jesus, really? Now I'm *really* suspicious. I assume you'll be around for another power breakfast soon enough."

Martin walked back into the lobby. It was obvious that he needed a meeting with Diop and quality one-on-one time with the major. He felt out of his depth and didn't mind admitting it. Maybe the conversation with Chlothilde had cleared away a few cobwebs. He called the major, who suggested lunch at an out-of-the-way spot near the airport.

•••

The major gave him a fierce handshake and arm grip. "Time for a summit. What say you?"

"I think so. *Know* so. Feeling out of the water, so to speak."

"Good first step to admit it. There aren't any textbooks or uni courses out there."

"Except for you."

"Okay, so I gather this is time for a serious natter. What's up, old cock?"

"A lot. Shall we start with the physical or the metaphysical?"

"Metaphysical. Always, always tricky."

"So . . . I've been thinking."

The major offered a sardonic smile. "One of the most feared sentences in the English language. About?"

"What am I doing here? I know—a little late in the day for that question, but that's not really it. The real question is where am I going after this little exercise?"

"Well, that's a bit of a deep one. The only easy answer I can give you is that only time will tell, and only you can decide. The reasons for the present exercise are fortunately more obvious: you're in a position to prevent a potentially major geopolitical crisis, put a truly nasty piece of work away, and extract some personal revenge."

"All in one neat, very dangerous bundle."

"I'll grant you dangerous, but it's unlikely to be neat. These things never are. However, you do have a serious personal stake in this."

"That's true, but I'm not in your line of work, part or full time."

"Nor should you be. I have a sense that you might feel too much. That can get in the way."

Martin was surprised by the comment. "Funny that. Someone just told me that I *think* too much and don't feel *enough*. The discussion was about moral absolutes. Speaking of which, what are yours?"

"The problem with that term is the 'absolute' bit. Life rarely leaves a fellow with black-and-white choices. Yes, there's absolute good, though about the rarest thing there is. Sadly, absolute evil is all too easy to find—as you know all too well. You've been next to it and smelled its breath."

Martin shuddered involuntarily. "For sure. And fucking choked the life out of it while I was at it."

"Have you lost any sleep over it since?"

"Not a bit."

"The problem, friend, is that most of life is lived in the gray zone. The ninety percent that sits between the black and the white. All you have then is your gut. That's where it all gets a bit dodgy or can."

"Back to no books or uni courses. How have you made those decisions when you've had to? Have you ever fucked up?"

"Not yet, but been close a few times. A couple of times I made the wrong decision, but fate or events intervened before I really made a hash of things."

"Second thoughts?"

"Sure, but I'm in a line of work that often requires very fast decisions. Second guessing is a luxury for the desk wallahs whose lives don't depend on these things. On the face of things, I'd have to say that your instincts seem pretty sound. My general rule of thumb, for what it's worth, is that most of us—the non-twisted types—have a built-in moral compass. If we do something wrong, it won't let us rest until we pay the piper. Whatever that looks like."

"So," Martin said, feeling a tinge of relief, "the fact that I'm not losing any sleep over my various encounters means I'm okay. Good to know. Speaking of which, I had one of my not-by-choice power breakfasts with Russell this a.m. He got down to some brass tacks, or we started to."

The major raised an eyebrow. "Do tell. Not that I trust him one little bit."

"Well, the money bit was easy enough: half down to a bank account of our choice. You notice I said *our*."

"Which means you don't have a discreet account."

"Nope. Figured you would. But that's the least of our problems. The real question is how we're going to keep him from shopping us before, during, or after the fact. Counting on your devious, wily mind for that. I thought of a dual signed confession to be held by both of us."

"Works in the books, not nearly enough in the real world, especially with a slippery bastard like Russell. We need a smoking gun with a much hotter barrel than that."

Martin had worried that would be the case. "Any ideas?"

"Don't worry. I'll come up with something. I have some ideas and some useful contacts."

"Well, not to be pushy, but the meter's running. Also, while you're rummaging around in your bag of tricks, what should I do when I grow up?"

The major chuckled. "That's one you'll have to answer when this chapter is over. Even if you have somewhat of an affinity for this stuff, I wouldn't suggest it as a full-time career. Plus, you've burned a remarkable number of bridges in a short time."

"True enough. Recently it seems like I'm beginning to wake up from a long nightmare."

The major fixed him with a steely-eyed stare. "Best you be awake. This is serious business, and there's no exit route for you, except through it."

"Don't worry, Major. I'm all in, no hesitation. Knew that when I got on the plane."

"You be fine, old cock. You've already seen off some pretty bad actors."

"Plus got someone who I loved killed."

"There's no easy answer for that," the major said with a sigh.

"I can only say that you were doing something that she wanted to happen. This is real-world stuff. It doesn't get much realer than here. Oddly and disturbingly poetic to be exploring our own inner darkness in the middle of the epicenter of a continent of darkness."

Martin shook his head. "You always surprise me, Major."

"Why? You didn't really think I was an automaton that went around doing this without a conscious thought. I do think. I do feel. I do hurt. And I've lost people. It stays with you, but no matter what you choose to do, if you don't take some risks somewhere along the line, you're going to be unfulfilled."

"I hear you, but all the time?"

"Please. The bulk of this job is observing and reporting."

"Until you run into the Russells of the world."

"News flash, young man. The Russells, Amins, and others who are even more unspeakably odious are in a strange way all about us. It's some of our jobs to minimize the harm that they can cause."

"Pretty thankless task."

"And the pay is highly inadequate if you're at all honest. Truth be told, you or I do it because someone has to. One thing to ponder given all the maladjusted types there are around: think how much worse things would be if we all just wandered around like sheep."

"I guess so, but it doesn't seem like much for the danger and risk."

"And boredom, and bullshit in spades. It can make a man think, but as you get older, you begin to take satisfaction in those times when the good guys come out on top."

Martin tried to adopt an optimistic tone. "Maybe I'll get there one day."

"You will, because you're already there; you just don't know it yet." The major stiffened his spine. "Now that we're done with the pep talk, we need to roll up our sleeves and do some serious planning."

"Agreed. We know enough now, and time is, well, shortening."

"So let's meet at Henri's tomorrow night. You have that concert tonight, right?"

"Yep, hot ticket. Le tout Kinshasa will be there. Aren't you going?"

"No, the perfect time to conduct some business quietly."

"Thanks for the chat and advice."

The major patted him on the back. "Please. Nothing you didn't already know. Sometimes we just have to hear it from others. Now off with you, and take bloody good care of my goddaughter."

• • •

Le tout Kinshasa was indeed out in force, and Henri hadn't disappointed with the tickets, which were for seats two rows behind Mobutu, Don King, and their respective entourages—and two rows in front of Ali, Foreman, and their respective entourages. The proverbial rock and a hard place. Both groups gave them questioning stares, as did many of the other celebrities in town for the fight. Mobutu let his gaze linger just enough to let them know he recognized them.

The music was extraordinary. The black American acts were feeling their roots. The crowd was soon dancing, Don King looking wooden and out of sorts, Mobutu rhythmic and graceful. Martin let the music take him away, away from Kinshasa, away from the recurring nightmare of the last year. His thought blurred into a slow-motion montage that ended as it always did: at the waterfall on Lamu.

"Cher." Chlothilde was gently shaking him. "*C'est fini.* Where were you?"

"Far away, but not long enough ago. Music does that for me. What a show." If only it was the music that was etched in his psyche.

"Cher, I will never forget this night."

If only I could, he thought as he guided her out through the animated throngs. Funny, he counted at least seven languages as they were carried along, but the music transcended the words and evoked a common response.

"Well, Martin, how'd you like the show? You got some pull. Your seats were a lot better than mine." Russell was always a buzz-kill. He had that sixth sense that allowed him to know exactly how to burst Martin's bubble.

"Just lucky, I guess, or having the right kind of friends. Not to mention not pissing certain folks off."

"The other night may be only the beginning. The fight has given our friend some temporary cover, but his arrogance may cost him."

"Coming from you, that's rich. It was a hell of a show—once in a lifetime."

"The fight will be too in ways some aren't imagining. Talk soon." Russell disappeared into the exiting crowd.

Chlothilde grimaced. "He is such a repulsive man and always around at the worst times."

"Too true," Martin replied, "and dangerous and mean as a snake to boot."

CHAPTER

16

THE NEXT DAY dragged. Martin had done all of the basic sight-seeing, and he hated the waiting. Too much time to think—never a good thing for him. Funnily enough, he didn't have the normal temptation during dead times to get a buzz on. The waves of grief had lessened as had the need to medicate them. He felt distinct relief when Hippolyte picked him up at six o'clock to go over to Henri's.

The group was there, the mood tense as the big fight grew nearer.

The major was all business. "All right, chaps, time to get to it. Monsieur Tshishkedi, when exactly is the shipment going to be moved?"

"It's timed to be going through town right as the fight begins," Etienne answered. "We wanted it to be optimum for our friend. I think we can assume that they will make their move on the east side nearest the airstrip."

"Probably, but he can be a canny bugger, so we'd best be prepared for anything. I would very much doubt, though, that he'll be with them."

Etienne nodded. "For sure. It's not his style to be involved personally."

"I presume your employer would prefer to have him caught red-handed."

"Naturalement, but how?"

Henri coughed. "That is the difficult question. Perhaps we force the Cubans to call him from the airport, claiming a last-second glitch."

The major pondered the idea. "That could work, but it would have to be good. He's a suspicious bastard."

"How about if they threaten to sell him out unless he pays more money?" Henri asked.

"That should go nicely. Of course, we'll have to have adequate manpower out there to deal with whatever folks he brings with him. Plus, he'll be loaded for bear." The major swirled his brandy in its snifter and took a serious puff on his punch before emitting three perfect smoke rings. "On the face of it, it's a start. However, it needs a lot of thinking and polishing. Henri, Etienne, what do you think your patron really wants out of this?"

"Certainement, he will want to use this to leverage the Amis for concessions." Etienne puffed and thought. "Clearly it is time that we revealed all this to him. We did not want to put everything on the table until we were sure. Especially with all of the commotion around the fight occupying him."

The major grinned, his eyes dancing. "I'd love to be a fly on that wall."

"It might be possible." Henri was smiling now too. "He knows you, and you have been useful to him in the past. Besides, he doesn't perceive the British as having a dog in this fight."

"That's true enough, though we do like to keep an eye on what the cousins are getting into. They have been known to wander off the reservation, to mangle a metaphor. When do you think this audience will take place?"

"Tomorrow without a doubt." Etienne rose. "I will call him. Of course, we will have to have the meeting somewhere discreet."

"That will be a trick in this town right now."

"Perhaps not. The president is supposed to visit Foreman's training camp outside of town tomorrow. Perhaps an unplanned but discreet detour could be arranged."

The major stood. "That's it then. We await your word. I assume it's a very small group for the meeting."

Etienne didn't bother answering, and everyone headed for the door.

Martin felt the familiar coppery taste of adrenalin in his mouth and the surge of energy. Nothing good had ever come of it, but he loved it so.

Chlothilde gave him an appraising look as they walked arm-in-arm to the long driveway. "Cher, you look like you are ready to fight."

"Is it that obvious?"

"Am I safe taking you home?"

"Probably." He flagged Hippolyte. "Fatal attraction: me and adrenalin."

Once back at the hotel, Martin couldn't sleep. He sat on the balcony watching Kinshasa's fidgety sleep. Truly it was a city that never relaxed—a perfect metaphor for his upcoming fortnight.

• • •

Hippolyte was waiting in the hotel lobby early the next morning. "Monsieur, your friend has instructed me where to take you. We must leave soon. Traffic will be bad, and we have to be there shortly."

He was right. Things were picking up for the fight. The traffic finally cleared about five miles out of the city center. Martin stared out the passenger window and saw nothing familiar. "Where are we, Hippolyte?"

"Near Nsele, Monsieur le President's compound. It is also where Foreman has his training compound."

"We aren't going there, are we?"

"Non, monsieur Martin, but somewhere close by."

It was clearly a pricey area of town. Spacious walled compounds dotted the wide streets. Many bristled with barbed wire or broken glass atop their thick cement walls.

Minutes later, they pulled into a walled compound that was crawling with heavily armed security. The guards appeared alert, their gleaming weapons locked and loaded

"Jeez, Hippolyte, this must be the place."

"Bien sur, all these Surete people make me nervous."

"There's certainly enough of them." Martin scanned the compound but saw no sign of Mobutu's heavily armored limousine.

Etienne emerged from the doorway of the house and waved him inside.

Martin exited the cab and turned to Hippolyte. "Stay cool. This isn't the hard part yet," he said hopefully before following Etienne into the luxuriously appointed villa. "Guesthouse?"

"In a way. When the president wishes to conduct very private meetings, he has several discreet establishments like this."

"How the other half lives."

"Monsieur Le President takes the affairs of state very seriously," Etienne said with a completely straight face.

Martin didn't even attempt to respond.

Etienne ushered him into a lux leopard-themed living room. Superb carvings and masks—not to mention large stuffed Oryx, Kudu, and other animal heads—hung from the walls on the walls. The place looked like a movie set. For all Martin knew, Mobutu had flown in someone to design the room. After all, he was reputed to keep a fully fueled and crewed 747 at the airport in case he and or any of his entourage wanted to fly to Paris for lunch and shopping.

US tax dollars at work.

"I say, old boy, your miles off."

Martin shifted his focus from the room to the major, who was ambling toward him with a smile on his face. "Just taking it all in."

"Well, best to come back down to Earth. His nibs will be here anytime, and we'll have to sing for our supper."

"'Tis true. Any ideas?"

"Well, old cock, this is one where we're going to have to play it as it lays. His nibs is a wily one."

"I look forward to observing two masters in action."

They didn't have long to wait. There weren't any sirens, but there might as well have been, even though Mobutu's motorcade was by his standards understated—only two motorcycles and the bulletproof Mercedes. Two door-sized bodyguards barged into the room and assumed standard ready positions by the door. Mobutu came in shortly after. Though Martin had sat at dinner with him, he hadn't realized how diminutive he was.

Etienne followed him and motioned them into seats once Mobutu had made his pick. Drinks weren't offered.

Message received, Martin thought. *Big-boy time. Time to do the brass-monkey thing and let the adults do the palavering.*

Mobutu got right to it. "This fellow Russell really is *tout a fait Americain* in all the worst ways. I forgot until dinner the other night."

"As you know, I, rather *we*," the major said, pausing to nod at Martin, "have had previous dealings with him. He is unsubtle, obnoxious—as in culturally tone deaf—but dangerous enough for all of that."

"Etienne informed me of the details of the events in Uganda. There was the matter of those missing diamonds. That nuisance Aka." Mobutu paused for effect and glanced at Martin.

"Yes, Monsieur le President," the major said, "but there was a woman involved as well."

Mobutu chuckled mirthlessly. "There almost always is."

The major, as always, was ready and slid effortlessly into the breach. "Monsieur le President, we all did things we lived to regret in our childhood, did we not? Martin really didn't understand anything about the local political situation, just how much he loved Mapende. Besides, he brought this to our attention and is going to play a key role going forward."

"So Etienne has led me to believe; otherwise, he wouldn't have survived dinner the other night." Mobutu shot Martin another steely glare. "He's young enough to make me believe that he followed his cock and not his brain, but Agent Russell, as you said, is a dangerous if unsubtle foe. Is he up to what we have in mind?"

"Monsieur Le President, he disposed of a rather nasty hench-man of Amin's named Bagaza."

"Bagaza. Where have I heard that name?"

"He was known to us. We used him a few times to clean up loose ends. A very nasty piece of business."

"D'accord. So, what is the situation?

"Russell has hired some Cubans to hijack the next shipment of Cobalt and Uranium from Shaba and sell it to the Libyans."

"*Merde alors!*" Mobutu slammed the table next to him, then visibly calmed himself. "Well, one has to admire his testicles if not his intelligence. Do we have a plan besides the obvious?"

"Monsieur le President, that's exactly what we're here to discuss. We do have several options as he's using Martin to do the smuggling."

"Curious that, *apres l'affair Aka*." Mobutu didn't bother to look at Martin; he'd already made his point.

"Quite, but the devil you know and all that."

"Yes, Major, as I recall, you tidied up all those loose ends rather well."

"Just a case of right place, right time."

Mobutu gave a small smile. "A fortunate habit of yours. What, do tell, are our options here?"

"Monsieur le President, it really depends on what you'd like to accomplish besides getting the uranium and cobalt to where they belong."

"One thinks there must be some interesting possibilities here, Major. Somehow, I am sure that you have thought about them."

"A few thoughts had occurred. It rather depends on what you'd like out of the situation."

"Certainement. The cobalt and Uranium must be delivered to the Amis at a bare minimum. Also, of course, I need to know who sold the information to Agent Russell on our side. Beyond that, l am not sure. I will certainly think of additional ways for my good friends to express their satisfaction."

"There might just be a much richer prize afoot."

"Why am I not surprised that you would have something up your sleeve, Major?"

"How about if you could offer our cousins the head of the Libyan nuclear program?"

"Merde alors, how?"

"Quite simple, really. The exchange is supposed to take place at an airstrip near the border with Chad. We just make sure it's the Chadean side. I've heard tell that you're close to Tombalbaye."

"We have had mutually agreeable dealings in the past."

"Quite, and you and I know his country hasn't been blessed with the natural resources that yours has—"

Mobutu finished the sentence. "And he would like a big slice of US aid. Yes, I think I see where your always devious mind is going."

"Not that devious, really. Cash for goods and human resources. A completely straight-forward exchange."

Martin was enjoying watching the two spiders weave their webs, but it was starting to get too close for comfort. "If I might interrupt, since this where it gets a little personal for me, am I hearing that we're going to let the hijack go ahead and then snatch the material back at the exchange in Chad?"

The major nodded. "Absolutely, old cock. Russell has got to think he's in control and that everything is going to plan. The Libyans will scamper right across the border if he doesn't give the signal. If we have all sorts of troops around, they won't come in."

"Yes, but he's going to have the Cubans with him at a minimum."

"Without a doubt, but Etienne and I will be waiting with a small group of special-force types. Additionally, the two pilots will be in our employ."

"So we let the original hijack succeed?" Mobutu got up and started to pace restlessly. "Thats a big risk."

The major appeared ready with his response. "But Friederich Tinner, the Swiss who is leading his nuclear weapons development effort, is a huge catch."

"You are, of course, right, mon ami."

Martin could almost see the wheels turning inside Mobutu's brain, and they all came up cash.

"Bien, Major. As usual, you have an ambitious plan. I think it can be done. The question is whether you think Mr. Fine is up to his piece in this."

Good point, Martin thought. He resented the fact that they were discussing him like he was a piece of meat. But truth be told, that was exactly what he was. The distance between the goat (the bait) and the leopard (the predator) was shrinking by the minute.

Once again, the major had a ready-made response. "He's here, isn't he? He wouldn't be if I didn't think he was up to it. Besides, he has a rather personal interest in this."

"Enlighten me, please."

"So," the major said, drawing out the word, "you know most of the Affair Aka, but as I said earlier, there was a woman involved."

"Yes, you mentioned that. It sounds like she was at the heart of things. Agent Russell never told me that, and I, of course, thought our friend here was just in it for the money." Mobutu cast a glance at Martin. "For me, revenge is the purest and most motivating of emotions. Love is too confusing and complicated for a simple fellow such as myself."

That was rich. Martin glanced at the major to see if the irony of the remarks had registered on him.

"Quite, Mr. President. Young Fine is highly motivated."

"Of that I now have no doubt, but he will need help—quite a bit of it. We all agree that while Agent Russell is unsubtle, he is not without talents, and I am sure he will have plenty of resources. This is not a small play."

"Agreed, but you also have many resources."

"As well as Etienne and you. Speaking of which, exactly what is your incentive in this?"

The major chuckled. "Well, certainly for starters, Her Majesty's government does not want the mad colonel to get his hands on nuclear weapons. I might also mention that my retirement is not far away."

"Bien sur, mon ami, you have frequently been of service. I am not a man who forgets these things. Once we finish this affair, you, Etienne, and I will discuss these matters. Now, unfortunately, I must attend a press conference with that cretin King." Mobutu rose, nodded at each of them, and strode out of the room without glancing back.

Etienne waited a moment before speaking. "Eh bien, Major, we have our marching orders. Where do we start?"

"Not from the beginning but the end. That's the tricky bit. How good are your relations with Tombolbaye's people?"

"Most excellent, assuming the price is right."

"Should be no problem, especially if we throw Tinner into the mix."

"Agreed, but how do we lure him in?"

"The mad colonel may be mad, but he isn't stupid. He will want to be sure of the goods' quality."

"Yes, but how do we get Tinner to come to Chad instead of an airfield just over the Libyan border? That is the proverbial—"

"Fly in the ointment. And that's just it: We will have to come up with a reason that the plane has to land in Chad, not Libya."

"How about a mechanical issue at the last minute?" Martin, having been cut out of most of the discussion so far, felt compelled to offer something, even if only to let them know he was there. After all, it was *his* ass on the line.

The major frowned as he mulled over the possibilities. "It's a thought, and it may be all we can do. The strip will have to be close enough that the Libyans see it as a piece of cake."

Etienne stood to leave. "We will have a few days to think about it. Now I will have to talk to my friends in N'Djamena about this upcoming affair. They are quite clever and may have some ideas, especially if it results in excess generosity from the Amis."

The major nodded. "I suspect you're right, and surely the Yanks will prefer snatching Tinner from Chad, though I'm sure he'll be well guarded. We'll have to think this out very carefully."

Martin rose and shook himself. "I can think of lots of scenarios—none of them simple or risk-free."

"Vraiment." Etienne guided them out into the blinding light. "This is a high-stakes game, but you knew that already."

Martin recalled his thoughts while drifting off to sleep the other night beside Chlothilde: *in for a penny*. Besides, he had his own early retirement to think about. "Major, can I drop you back in town?"

"Yes, time we had a bit of a chat, anyway."

•••

The major waited until they were well underway to start. "Second thoughts, old boy?"

"I'd like to live to be an old boy—and by the way, a rich one, or at least richer than I am right now. This is getting complicated."

"Of course. It was always going to. We're not just smuggling diamonds here."

"Obviously, but Tinner too—that's definitely upping the ante."

"Absolutely, and the payoff. Besides, if things play out the way I think they will, your friend Agent Russell might get his just desserts from the mad colonel. He's not known for tolerating failure."

"There's that, but aren't we going to be putting our faith and trust in a bunch of unknown partners?"

"To some extent, but I trust Etienne with my life. Already have several times, as a matter of fact. He's a cool customer, and more importantly, absolutely ruthless."

"That's encouraging, I think. You confident of his men?"

"I'm confident he'll pick good ones."

"What about Russell's folks?"

"Cubans, probably. They'll be battle tested. We'll have to spring our trap well. Of course, the joker in the pack could be the Chadians, but they've been fighting a vicious civil war for donkey's years."

"And I get to sit in the middle and watch. Just kidding. But it does make a man think."

"All in the planning, old bean. We just need to get the jump on them. That said, we're going to need something a lot better thought out and organized than what we have in hand right now. That's where Etienne and I will have to earn our big bucks."

"Do tell."

"Well, I'm inclined to think we need to take a flight from our little bolt hole here to whatever strip Etienne's folks have in mind and do a little in-situ planning. I'm never comfortable without knowing the exact lay of the land."

"Besides, we'll be able to get some sense of our potential partners."

"That too. We should probably get out in the next few days. The fight is nine days away. That's enough time if we don't dawdle. Drop me at my digs, and we'll meet Etienne in the AM to plan things out. You might want to wine-and-dine that goddaughter of mine. She's a handful at times, but she likes you—God knows why."

Martin chuckled to himself. That was as close to affection as the major ever got. But Martin's smirk faded as he reflected on how serious the situation was becoming. His thoughts hardened into reality during the ride into town with the major, and Martin felt the acid of adrenaline-based fear churn in his stomach. How he loved and hated it, but he also knew he was too far in to get out now. Things had gone quiet with the major, and he forced his thoughts elsewhere until Hippolyte dropped them off.

Martin went up to his room and called Chlothilde, who was eager to see him. *Thank God for charming distractions*, he thought as he showered.

• • •

Hippolyte dropped Martin at Chlothilde's just in time for a dip and some champagne while the sun set.

Chlothilde sipped from her champagne flute. "So, Martin, I am bursting with curiosity, and the time for the fight is getting close. What are you and my always devious godfather up to? It's okay. He and Henri talked after you came back."

Martin ran down where they were.

Chlothilde sighed and shrugged. "It seems very—how shall I say?—disorganized."

"I agree, but hopefully after we fly up to Chad and talk to Etienne's friends up there, things will get more focused. The thing that scares me a little is that the situation is going to be fluid. The plan is unlikely to survive the first shot, so to speak."

"I certainly hope there are no shots."

"Me too. A figure of speech. Still, it's likely to get exciting before it's over."

"You must be careful. Russell is a bit crazy, you know."

"I *do* know, but sadly, crazy like a fox. I'm counting on the major being smarter."

"He always is, but these things never go according to plan, as you said. Two of my favorite men will be in peril." She hugged him fiercely.

"A little or lot of luck wouldn't hurt, either."

17

HIPPOLYTE PICKED HIM up at nine the next morning and shuttled him to yet another non-descript storefront in a part of town he'd never been to. Etienne seemed to have plenty of bolt holes around town. No surprise to Martin, but the man had things wired—at least in Kinshasa. Sadly, that was only half of the battle.

Etienne and the major were already hunched over a large table with a detailed map in front of them.

The major was the first to greet him. "Welcome, Martin. What do you know about the Aouzou Strip?"

"Nothing."

"Well, come over and take a look, because it's going to be important in the scheme of things." The major beckoned him over and pointed to a strip between the Chadian and Libyan outlined in red pencil.

"Pardon my ignorance, but which country is it in? Your markings have covered the border."

"That's just it, mon ami." Etienne tapped the map for emphasis. "It depends on who you talk to. Our friend Monsieur le President Tombalbaye claims it as part of Chad. However, the good colonel claims there is an old treaty deeding it to Libya. There is only one problem: No one seems to be able to find a copy. Sadly a typically African arrangement."

Martin glanced up from the map. "How inconvenient for him, but the colonel isn't the sort to take a minor setback like that seriously."

"Quite, old boy. That's why he keeps Frolinat around. They're a 'liberation movement,' whose sole aim is to liberate the strip from the Chadians. I probably should add that there are reputed to be uranium reserves and oil under the sand, but no one has verified that."

"So, let's see . . . There's us, Frolinat, Russell, Tombalbaye, and the mad colonel. That should be easy to sort out."

"Don't panic. This is a huge, empty area that no one really controls. We need to pick our spot and timing. Etienne, can we count on Tombalbaye for support? I mean *real* support. Tombalbaye will be with us, yes?"

Etienne nodded. "Certainement. He despises the colonel, but Frolinat and the Libyans will be with Agent Russell."

"How close are relations with Tombalbaye's people?"

"As close as they need to be, but as you know, Chad is a poor country, so money always helps."

"Quite. So the thought occurs: What if we offered them the chance to catch Tinner and sell him to the cousins? No need to worry. I'm sure they'll be willing to show their appreciation to all of us for such a big catch."

Etienne leaned back from the map. "That all sounds good, of course, but we all know it's not going to a simple exercise. We need a good reason for the plane to land in the strip and not over the border in Libya to start with."

"That really shouldn't be that hard. It's a very long flight—eight hours plus. What aircraft do you have in mind?"

"A perfect one: an old Antonov we seized from some gun runners about two years ago."

"Hmm . . . That could be really useful, but from what I can recollect, Antonovs don't have the range for the flight."

"With extra fuel tanks barely, perhaps, but too risky. There is no place safe to refuel, either."

The major looked pleased. "Well, there it is. We have to land in the strip. Too big a chance otherwise."

"That could work well, mon ami. With Frolinat around and the Libyans who frequently slip over the border into the strip, Agent Russell should be comfortable enough to buy that."

The major turned to Martin. "That's your job. We'll supply the pilots, of course, and you'll convince Russell it won't be difficult. Also, Agent Russell's client will, I'm sure, want Tinner to confirm that he's not being taken for a ride. Of course, we'll now have to let things play out. No more hijacking the hijacking. So more variables in play, but bagging Tinner is huge."

Etienne, like the major, appeared satisfied. "D'accord. Things are beginning to shape up. Martin, I suggest that you take a commercial flight to N'Djamena tomorrow, as I am sure Russell will be informed. I will book the tickets today. The major and I will take a more discreet form of travel so as not to arouse suspicion."

"One night, right?" Martin wanted to be sure. "I assume you'll book the hotel too."

"Yes, I will put you in the obvious one, and you can play the tourist. The major and I will stay elsewhere. We can't be too careful."

"I'm assuming you'll make the arrangements for the meet."

"Yes, the tickets will be with Hippolyte. He will tell you the hotel name and give you a password that your contact will use. It is important to realize that the Amis have lots of assets in N'Djamena because of its relative proximity to Libya. As I recall, the flight to

N'Djamena leaves mid-morning, so be ready by eight. Give me your passport, and I will take care of the visa this afternoon when I am making the other arrangements."

The major rose. "Good. Lots to do. Let's get cracking. Martin, a few things to know about N'Djamena . . . It's one of the hottest cities in the world. This time of year, the highs will push a hundred and fifteen degrees."

• • •

Martin rode back to the hotel on his own, alone with his thoughts. Things were moving fast—faster than he'd expected—and he was flying blind. A disconcerting thought. At least in Uganda he'd been on the ground for a good bit.

He knew next to nothing about Chad. Hopefully he wouldn't be there long enough for it to matter much.

He ate an early dinner alone and took himself up to bed. Who knew what tomorrow would bring?

CHAPTER

18

Hippolyte picked Martin up at eight o'clock sharp and handed him a fat envelope once they were on the road to the airport. "Everything is in there. Your flight leaves at ten-thirty. When you land in N'Djamena, take a car to the Novotel check-in and wait in the lobby. Someone will approach you and say Lamu is a long way away."

All suitably cloak-and-daggerish, Martin thought to himself, but then again, he was a rank amateur working with two pros, and history had taught him to show a healthy respect for Russell's capacity for violence as well as his resources.

The three-hour flight passed quickly. He dozed off for most of it before the bumpy landing jarred him awake. The landscape through the window looked a lot drier than Kinshasa.

A solid wall of dry heat slapped him in the face when the stewardess opened the door. The major hadn't been kidding about the heat. The airport was quiet, as it should have been since N'Djamena wasn't exactly on the Bwana safari circuit. Immigration formalities were quick, and Martin was impressed that there were no hidden costs. That was unusual for Africa. Not so the taxis, whose drivers were as rapacious as any Martin had encountered. It took him twice as long to negotiate the ride price as it had to clear the formalities.

The ride to the Novotel was quick and uninteresting, N'Djamena was flat, dusty and dry. It had the torpor that always seemed to afflict hot places. Everyone was moving slowly. It was so hot that the air shimmered. Martin didn't think he'd ever been in a hotter place before. Mercifully, it was so arid the sweat dried on him before it could stain his shirt.

The hotel was shiny and new for Africa, but the desk service was slow and traditional Africa. He chided himself. What was he in a hurry for? But the adrenal acid in his gut and the familiar coppery taste in his mouth told him all he needed to know. He dumped his bag in the room, glancing around just long enough to notice it was bog-standard modern with almost no African personality, and headed back down to the bar area off the lobby.

The bar at least made a minimal effort at African atmosphere, complete with phony leopard-skin bar stools with matching banquettes. He ordered the local lager Gala, which, like most beers in Africa, was really good and really cold. One positive colonial legacy: good beer everywhere.

He was halfway through the beer when an African slid into the chair opposite him and extended his hand. "Sorry for the intrusion. My name is Hasan Dibre, and you are a long way from Lamu." His English was good, but Martin detected that partial French intonation that all Francophone speakers had. "I have a car outside to take us to the meeting."

Martin paid up and followed him out to a waiting Peugeot. Hasan waved him into the front seat, and they set off through sparse traffic.

"First time in N'Djamena?"

"Yes, so far it's hot and dusty."

"That's true most of the time," Hasan said, smiling. "We are going a little out of town where it is nicer. We will be near the river. I presume that you know the other side is Cameroon?"

"Yes, I did, but I haven't been to this part before. Am I allowed to ask where we're going and who we're seeing?"

"Yes, of course. We are going to the house of Colonel Deby, on the Chari River. Colonel Deby is the Commandant of the DDS, the Directerate de Documentation and Security. He is my commandant."

Well, that figured. Best to go in at the top.

It was a thirty-minute drive alongside the Chari, a turgid brown river that meandered through a greener landscape than N'Djamena. Martin remembered from the maps that it joined another river, the Logone, then connected to Lake Chad. It seemed cooler—but not by much.

They pulled up to a modern bungalow about thirty minutes later. Five or six guards, alert and armed to the teeth, walked the perimeter.

Hasan led them him inside to a large living room dominated by a circular glass table with Cape Buffalo hooves as feet. Everyone seemed to like movie set decoration. Or was this just the real deal? Etienne, the major, and a tall African wearing a bunch of ribbons and medals sat around the table.

"Mr. Baker, I presume, or can we dispense with that, Mr. Fine? Welcome, I am Colonel Deby." He motioned for Martin to take a seat. "You know everyone else."

Etienne passed a carafe of cold water over to him. "We were just having a most interesting chat with the colonel. He has had dealings with Agent Russell in the past."

"Yes," the colonel said. "I never really trusted him. Now I am worried about what he may be betraying to Gaddafi and the Frolinat. Merde alors, I will be glad to be rid of him—permanently would be even better."

"Monsieur le Colonel, let's start with messing up his current plans. No guarantees he'll be accompanying the shipment. Not like him to be that close to the action." The major rose and pointed to the map. "What do we have in the way of options for a landing strip in the strip?"

"What sort of plane are we talking about?"

"Antonov AN9."

"That limits our choices, but there will still be a few." Colonel Deby hunched over the map with a red pencil. He appeared to think for a moment before circling two locations. "These could both do. They are in the strip close enough to the border for our purposes but not currently controlled by Frolinat."

The major studied the map closely. "They both look to be about twenty to thirty clicks on our side. What sort of force can you bring to bear up there?"

"What do we need?"

"Hard to say, Colonel. We have to assume that if we lure Tinner over there, it will be considerable. He's a huge asset."

"Of course. Plus, we will have to manage things after dark as the Libyans will have chopper support at a minimum. I think I can lay my hands on some useful assets for that. And if we have a word with our real friends amongst the cousins, they will give us what we need to get the job done."

"No troops."

"Of course, the cousins wouldn't anyway, but they don't want the mad colonel getting the goods. They have some bloody useful handheld missiles these days. Nothing like a shooting war to develop stuff."

"How are you going to persuade the Libyans to come to us and bring Tinner also?" the major asked.

"We'll just have to sweeten the pot a bit."

Etienne got up and stretched. "I must admit, Major, I have

been asking myself that question too."

"Well, I think a whisper in the right place that there might be some natural plutonium-240 in the shipment might just do the trick."

"But we haven't found any yet."

"Agent Russell doesn't know that, and it's the holy grail. It would take years off the Libyan effort. Plus, it's not as simple as sticking a Geiger counter next to it to see if it's real. Give the agent a whiff of that, and he'll come running. So will Professor Tinner."

Etienne nodded. "You are right. The perfect coup de main. I think know exactly how we can bait the trap."

"I sort of thought you would." The major turned to Martin. "Are you following this?"

"More or less. The easy part of the fuel thing is to force a landing this side of the border. Once we're down, I'm wondering how much cavalry we'll need to deal with Russell and the Libyans. Remember: I'll be flying in blind with hot cargo and Cubans all over me like a cheap suit."

"Quite, old boy. Don't worry. I haven't forgotten."

"Nor I." Etienne started pacing. "We have to have a simple but foolproof plan."

"Etienne, my friend," the major said, "we need a simple plan, with two or three backup scenarios. The only thing for sure is that things will not go exactly to plan. They never do."

"That's encouraging."

The major rose. "Better reality than a phony pep talk. Gentlemen, next steps?"

"I will start looking into the arrangements here," Colonel Deby said as he, too, stood. "Etienne, as soon as you have baited the trap in Kinshasa, I will do a little salting of my own up here. Plus," he said, pausing to wink at the major, "I will start planning our little reception when you land. Who will put the Americans in the loop? They, as you might imagine, given who's next door, have a large establishment here."

The meeting was coming to an end.

"Martin, we'll depart separately as we can't be seen with you, and there are many eyes around town." The major patted him on the shoulder. "I suggest you hit a few of the local haunts around town before your flight home tomorrow. Your presence will be noticed. There aren't many tourists around N'Djamena."

Martin felt like he'd barely had time to absorb anything. But the pace was accelerating, which meant he had no choice but to keep up. "Okay, I'm sure that the good colonel will tell me where to go to best be seen by the right folks."

"You won't have to go far. The boite in your hotel is the hot spot these days. Everyone who is watching anyone will be there."

• • •

Hasan drove Martin back to the hotel, and Martin showered, dined, and went to the club. It was the normal African nightclub mélange. Ladies of the night, expats, diplomats, aide folks—all drinking and dancing to the latest Parisian pop and speaking with lilting Congolaise. Martin had a few beers and played spot the spotter. There were plenty of likely candidates, and some of them were bound to be on the right payrolls. He took himself off to bed tired but felt no more confident that they had a workable—or, for that matter, *any*—plan.

CHAPTER

19

HIPPOLYTE PICKED MARTIN up at the airport. Things were definitely revving up for the fight. The city was jammed with obvious fight types.

"Town is really jumping," Martin said as they pulled up to the hotel.

"Bien sur. Only a little more than a week. I do not recall seeing the ville this crowded with so many tourists."

He wasn't kidding. Martin had to thread his way through the hotel lobby. There were long lines of frustrated folks experiencing African efficiency.

Martin showered, unpacked, and called Chlothilde, who invited him over to her place. She sounded eager to hear about everything.

When he arrived, she interrogated him at the front door. "How was the trip?"

"Quick. Wish I could say the plan was any clearer, but at least I think I've finally met all the important players."

"But surely you must know more now."

"The outlines and players are pretty clear, but not the mechanics. Sadly, they won't be clear until after we pull the trigger. Sorry, bad pun there, I hope."

135

Worry lines appeared on her forehead. "You are kidding! Joking about a thing like this!"

"It's no joke, just reality. This is a fluid deal. There's no precisely tailored script. Wouldn't matter if there was. It would be toast the minute things started."

"Merde, explain."

"Too many moving parts. We don't know how many men Russell will have for the hijack for starters. That's not such a big deal, since no one is planning to resist, anyway. Once we land up in Chad, who the hell knows what's going to happen."

"I can't believe that you just said that. What are you not telling me?"

"Everything that hasn't been told to me." He gave her a gentle kiss. "Okay, really, I'm sure that the major, Etienne, and our new best friend in N'Djamena, Colonel Deby, are hatching something. I'll be told in due time on a need-to-know-basis."

She led him inside. "I have some very important need-to-know information, but it's only for us."

CHAPTER

20

THE INCESSANT RINGING of the phone woke Martin abruptly the next morning. He glanced at his watch. It was 6:45 a.m. Couldn't be anyone he wanted to talk to.

"Good morning, pretty boy. Rise and fucking shine. Lobby in fifteen."

Martin was hazy. The voice sounded vaguely then ominously familiar. "Jesus, Russell, really?"

"Party is soon. Time to start planning. Come down ready. We'll be away for a chunk of the day."

Martin ejected out of bed into the shower and was down in the lobby suited and booted twenty minutes later.

Russell was sitting at a table with the two Cubans Martin had met the week before. They were as suitably tough-looking as he remembered.

Russell handed Martin a plastic cup of coffee. "Not bad for an amateur. Your taste seems to run black in most things, presumably in your coffee too. Hope you appreciate the concierge service."

Martin suppressed the urge to hammer Russell. Hopefully his day would come. "Appreciate it, Steve. Nice to see my tax dollars at work."

Russell and his posse led Martin outside to a well-used Rover at the curb.

"Make yourself comfortable," Russell said. "We've got a bit of a ride in front of us."

Comfortable it was not. The Rover was old and funky. The cracked upholstery discharged a vague fugue of body odor mixed with dust, all enveloped in the now familiar Kinshasa scent of rotting garbage, wood smoke, and a vague hint of sewage.

They meandered through morning rush-hour traffic for a half hour or so until they approached a lightly populated section on the outskirts of the city. The car pulled off to the side of the road. They sat for a few minutes, Russell and his posse intently observing the traffic, which was negligible at that hour.

"Part one," Russell said. "See that dirt road on the left? That's where you'll divert the truck to. You can be parked there while the others stop the truck."

"What do we do with the guards?" one of Russell's goons asked.

"You know what to do."

"Si, Jefe."

Well, that was fucking reassuring, Martin thought. No doubt they'd know what to do with him at the appropriate time too, but that was where the major and Etienne came in—or had better. It also reinforced the need to land in the strip and not Libya proper, which in turn meant that Martin had better get to know a little more about the Antonov AN9.

Russell interrupted his thoughts. "So, Mr. Fine, where are we with the transport?"

"All set. One slightly-used-but-none-the-worse-for-wear Antonov AN9 will be waiting fully fueled and ready to go. Including two experienced pilots. They've run just about everything into every country round these parts that you can think of. Extra fuel tanks laid on, but it's going to be close."

"You'd better be sure, buddy. Unauthorized stops will be strictly verboten."

"Understood. I'm sewing up the final arrangements tomorrow. We still going fight night?"

"For sure. No one will be paying attention to anything else."

"Hate to miss it, but I'll get over it."

"I can think of a few thousand reasons why. We're going back out to HQ to make the final plans."

Everyone was quiet on the ride out to the so-called HQ. Plenty to think about.

Upon arrival, Russell waved them inside toward the rickety table and spread a large ordinance map on it. He circled an area with a red pencil. "Ground zero where you take the shipment." He drew a somewhat circular route, avoiding the central part of Kinshasa, and circled another spot. "Matete. We'll make a few practice runs to get our timing down, but I figure no more than thirty to forty minutes with everyone occupied elsewhere."

"What time are you figuring?" Martin asked.

"Well, the fight doesn't start until around four a.m.. Remember: it's got to be on during prime time in the US."

"How long do you think we'll have before they raise the general alarm?"

"Well, it's normally about a three-hour run from the mine to the storage bunker. Figure they're about halfway in when the boys here do the hijack. Another forty-five to the strip. You should be in the air for at least forty-five minutes to an hour by the time they start getting worried. Then they'll mess around a while. This is Africa, after all."

"Plenty of time even in an Antonov to get out of Zairian airspace."

"No worries there. I can assure you that the Zairian air force has zero capability of troubling you if you fly low. They don't have the radar, the planes, or the pilots to do so."

Martin exhaled slowly. "On the face of it, a relatively safe operation. Wish I believed it would be that simple, but it never is."

"Come on, Fine. You'll have the bases covered better than last time, if you learned anything."

Hopefully, he thought to himself.

Russell led them around back to where a large truck was parked. It looked pretty new, complete with Zairean military markings.

"More of our tax dollars at work?" Martin asked.

"Shit yeah. We borrowed it for a few days, but they'll get it back at Matete. Consolation prize."

"I'm sure they'll be thrilled. I wish I was going to be around to see your what-a-surprise acting job."

"It will be the best that the colonel's dinars can buy."

"No doubt, so I won't be seeing you after Matete."

"I sincerely hope not for both of our sakes."

Martin didn't bother to respond. Russell hadn't been sincere about anything for so long he probably didn't know the difference. "There is one matter: my insurance."

"I was wondering when you were going to get to that." Russell pulled an envelope out of his pocket. "See if this will do."

Martin skimmed it quickly. It covered all the bases—and confirmed to him that Russell planned to have him killed. "Looks like it will do."

"Good. Hand it back over. You don't get it until just before you shut the plane door at Matete. Can't have it floating around until the deal goes down, can we?"

He had a point, but Martin wasn't sure where that left him. Definitely an issue for the major to sort out.

Russell waved them to the car. "Your assignment is to be waiting at Matete at three-thirty a.m., no later, fully fueled, and ready to go on fight night. Got it? If anything changes between now and then, I'll be in touch."

They left the minders at the camp. It was a quiet ride back to town. Martin saw no reason to chat with Russell. The atmosphere of hate and mutual distrust was so thick it was oppressive. He felt a huge wave of relief when they got back to the hotel.

Russell scowled at him. "I don't have to tell you not to do anything stupid, do I?"

Martin gave him a mock salute and went up to his room. He felt out on a limb. There was nothing certain in his mind except Russell being out to screw him—and everyone else, for that matter. He collapsed on his bed and drifted off to a restless sleep.

• • •

Martin awoke to the sound of the phone ringing. It was dark out.

The major greet him on the other end of the line. "Hippolyte is downstairs to bring you here."

"Where's *here*?"

"Chlothilde's. We're all having dinner and a meeting."

"Okay, that's reassuring after I spent the greater part of the afternoon with our good buddy Russell going over his plans."

Martin showered and was climbing into the old Peugeot ten minutes later. "You miss me, Hippolyte?"

"Bien sur, mon amie. Life is quiet without you."

"Even with the fight?"

"Monsieur, all they want to do is drink and go upstairs with the women."

"Sounds about right."

• • •

Full fucking house, as it should be, Martin thought to himself after arriving at Chlothilde's place. The only one missing was Mobutu himself. They were all in the dining room huddled around the major's previously marked-up map.

"The first question," Etienne said, "is how are we going to handle the hijack?"

"That one's easy, old man," the major answered. "We won't handle it at all. We want the buggers to have it. No fuss, no muss. Your men must hand the truck over without a fight. Same with the escorts."

Etienne nodded. "Of course, I just worry about Russell's men. "

"I'm confident they'll be experienced and under orders to keep it clean, quiet, and quick. He's using Cubans who've been on the ground here for a while. No problems with them. How about your chaps?"

"I will have my best for here and the other end. Deby is also assigning his most experienced men, so we are good there. All that said, we really haven't focused on the back end, which we all know will be the trickiest and riskiest."

"Quite. Any word from Deby on what strip we're planning on using?"

"Yes, it should be right here." Etienne rotated the map toward him and pointed to a small dot. "Yes, there it is: Enery Conou."

"Looks suitably isolated," Martin said.

The major chuckled. "Bloody desert, old boy."

"How far from the Libyan border?" Martin asked.

"My guess is thirty to forty clicks." Etienne used his fingers against the scale measure on the map. "In any case, it's the location that Deby selected. He must have a good reason."

"Makes sense." The major rotated the map back toward him. "Close enough to the Libyan border that Russell and cronies won't be too uptight. I'm presuming Frolinat is around those parts too."

Etienne nodded. "They move around, as you know, but one must assume Deby thinks he can lock down that area for long enough."

"Finally, we get down to it." Martin started pacing. "I've been dying to know. What the hell happens when we land?"

"Not being difficult, Martin, but there are a lot of moving parts to that piece of the tale." The major motioned them all to sit down. "Let's start at the beginning. How are we going to get the big prize—Herr Tinner—there?"

"Your original idea of baiting the trap with some plutonium-240 seemed a good way to go to me," Martin said.

"Talk is cheap, and Russell's no fool." The major turned to Etienne. "Is it time to let the cat out of the bag?"

"Certainement. If not now, when?"

The major seemed to be studying Martin. "How much do you know about nuclear weapons?"

Martin couldn't believe his ears. "Really, Major?"

"Thought so. Well, the basics are uranium, as I am sure you know, plus another fissile material that can be fused together by a normal explosion to split the atoms and release exponentially greater energy than the elements would individually."

"With you so far."

"So Zaire has plenty of Uranium—we all know that—but it also happens to have the magic extra ingredient to make things glow in the dark, so to speak. Plutonium-240, old boy. The mad colonel would kill for it."

"Okay, so what makes it so special and valuable to him?"

"It has to be produced in a nuclear reactor, and Zaire is the only country on the continent that has one."

"No kidding. How did that happen? It seems an odd choice."

The major smiled. "Not if you know the history. Where do you think the US got the uranium for those first nuclear weapons they used in World War Two? It wasn't in the US, though it was discovered there later. It came from here. The Yanks did a deal with the Belgians. Uranium in return for a reactor, which they duly built here in 1958."

Martin sat back, impressed. "Well, I'll be. That's a pretty obscure piece of history, but I'm sure the colonel knows all about it."

"Bien sur." Etienne chuckled mirthlessly. "We have two Libyan agents being entertained by our Surete as we speak. That may suit our purposes, as we just spent a lot of money upgrading the reactor, which had fallen into disrepair. I do believe the Amis footed the bill. That's handy. No doubt Agent Russell has reported this to the colonel."

"Counting on it," the major said. "That's the bait for the Libyans and Tinner. The colonel will want Tinner to vet the goods, especially since plutonium-240 is hard to identify. He will also know that Mobutu had it renovated and updated recently to produce more plutonium for the Amis."

"Okay, so we can assume Russell has already talked to the colonel." Martin looked at the map and jotted down a few notes. "Nothing to it. We bait the trap ,and he and Tinner show up to meet the plane. Then we bag the cat, the mouse, and the cheese—all in one fell swoop."

"Pretty much."

"A few minor details, if you will," Martin said. "We're going to need to refuel the Antonov, for one thing. That's going to take some time if we have to do it by hand. That means securing the perimeter for a chunk of time. Etienne, you'll have that covered, right?"

"We will. I will make sure that we have adequate resources to cover that. My patron is expecting a big payoff from the Amis for his services."

The major rolled up the map. "No doubt he'll get one. This is a big deal on many levels."

Etienne eyed the major. "What about you?"

"Well, retirement is out there sometime soon, as I'm sure your boss appreciates."

"He appreciates it greatly. You have done many good things for him. However, neither he nor I see you retiring any time soon."

"True enough. What would I possibly do with myself? Can't see myself lolling on the beach somewhere. Bloody boring."

The man had a point, Martin thought and chuckled to himself. The major would be scheming right until he hit St Peter, and even then, he'd have something figured. "What's next, folks?"

"Logistics, reserves, and planning." The major slapped the table for emphasis. "Most campaigns fail before a shot is fired due to lack of or poor staff work. It's not happening here, especially because this will be a complicated op with lots of moving parts."

"Where do I fit in?" Martin asked. "More than happy to pull my own weight, but this isn't exactly my home turf."

"Quite. Etienne, how about if you put Martin in touch with the pilots and let him sort the transport issues?"

"D'accord, Major. I presume you and I will handle the details of the operation in Chad with Colonel Hasan."

"That's our territory. Martin, I suggest that you and my goddaughter continue to play the just-here-for-the-fight routine. There may be other folks besides our buddy Agent Russell watching things. Lots of people are interested in Zaire these days."

Etienne stood to leave. "Martin, Hippolyte will pick you up at the hotel at nine tomorrow. You will make a highly visible trip out to Matete. I am sure Monsieur Russell will have eyes on you. There will be a fellow named Lucienne who will have the answers we need regarding the transport."

"Mercie bien," Martin said. "Shall we reconvene day after tomorrow here?"

"Good plan. Now let's get cracking. We have a busy week ahead of us." The major ushered them outside. "Martin, if you're not already doing this, pay attention to whoever is tailing you. Don't try to lose them."

"They've been easy enough to spot. Figured you'd want me to keep them in sight. If I drop them, we might get the A team."

"Someone taught you well."

"Not touching that one."

"Off with you, and take good care of Chlothilde."

CHAPTER

21

HIPPOLYTE WAS PUNCTUAL as usual the next morning, and they headed north out of town. Martin hadn't traveled in that direction before, and he could see why it wasn't on the tourist routes. Just a few miles out of the city center, a massive urban sprawl of mud huts with rusted zinc roofs took over from the relatively affluent centre ville. The slums were as miserable as any Martin had ever seen. He wrinkled his nose at the overpowering stench of raw sewage and rotting garbage.

"Kibera is not a nice place," Hippolyte said, stating the obvious.

"How many live there?"

"Hard to say, monsieur. They come for a better life and end up with a worse one. We know the gods are not fair, but they are unfairest of all if you live in Kibera."

It was hard to argue the point. The inhabitants were mostly loitering about with the same wide-eyed stare Martin had seen in other hopeless places. They were zombified on life support.

After several minutes, the slums gave way to more open country and fresher air.

"How much further to Matete?" Martin asked.

"About twenty minutes. It is very isolated."

No surprises there.

147

Martin hung on as the road rapidly deteriorated into the African-bush norm. Hippolyte was an expert driver, but even still, Matin felt like he was in a cement mixer during several patches. "You weren't kidding," he said, grunting as they swung off onto a track that could barely be called a road.

Two bone-jarring minutes later, a couple of seasoned-looking characters stepped out of the bush and waved them to a halt with their Ak-47s.

Hippolyte said a few words to them, and they were waved through.

"You've been here a few times before?"

"Many."

They pulled up in front of a large rusted hangar. There was a hulking transport plane inside. It had to be an Antonov, Martin thought, although he couldn't say for sure.

A tall, gangly African came out. "Martin, Lucienne. Etienne told me you'd be out. I'm the pilot, and there's the plane. She's old but dependable."

Martin walked around the battered, oil-streaked plane. It didn't inspire confidence at first glance. "Good enough to get us where we're going?"

"In her sleep. Remember: It's my life too."

"Point taken. What about fuel? It's a long way up there."

"Yes, four to five hours flying time. If we had heavy cargo, it would be a problem. We will certainly have to refuel up there."

"How long will that take? We may not have a lot of time."

"With a truck, not too bad: twenty to thirty minutes. Without . . ." Lucienne shrugged. No further answer required or offered.

"Then a truck had better be laid on."

"It will be. Lucienne has done this before, many times."

"Comforting as that may be, I don't want to be you're first screw-up. There aren't going to be any do-overs on this one."

"It will be fine. I will have everything ready in a week's time. When will we be taking off?"

"Sometime between ten and midnight would be my guess, but I wouldn't be surprised if it's later. Just be ready. You know how these things roll out."

"I will be ready—you can be sure." Lucienne gave him a mock salute. "You take care of your affairs. I will be responsible for mine."

The ride back to town was silent until Martin asked Hippolyte, "Is Lucienne as experienced as he seems? He's very confident and laid back."

"He has done this for many years, no problems."

They reached the hotel a half an hour later. Obviously, some big event was taking place. The entrance was swarming with paparazzi and hangers-on.

"They must have heard I was coming," Martin quipped.

"Mais non, not you. That looks like James Brown, le Roi du Soul. See him getting out of the car?"

No shit, Martin thought. It was impossible to miss the pompadour 'do anywhere. "Christ, are they all staying here?"

"Certainement. Where else?"

Where else indeed? Martin thought for a second. *Maybe not such a bad thing, all in all.* The general commotion would divert attention away from him.

Hippolyte bid him adieu. "I will be back for you at six, Monsieur Martin. There is a dinner meeting at Monsieur Henri's this evening."

Martin pushed his way through the packed lobby. One thing was for sure: No one was interested in him. No wonder every big soul and R&B act was piling into town for the week-long festival! *What a circus*, he thought. Somehow it seemed a fittingly surreal wraparound to the serious business at hand. That old African feeling of being in a movie without the cameras rolled over him again.

. . .

The gang, including their new best friend, Colonel Deby, was all there when Martin walked into Henri's a few hours later.

"Welcome, Martin. We can kick on now." The major waved him to a seat.

Henri offered around cigars and gestured toward the bar. Game time. There weren't any takers.

As was his want, the major took charge. "Right, folks. Now it gets serious. Colonel, nice to meet you. Heard good things."

"Likewise, Major. Your reputation proceeds you always."

The major laughed. "Now that we have that poppycock out of the way, brass tacks. What's the situation at the proposed rendezvous? They are lots of questions. Frolinat first. How thick will they be on the ground?"

"They have some presence, as you know, in the border areas," Deby answered, "but we can secure the strip no problem. Besides, the other colonel will not want to endanger the exchange."

"Quite, as long as they get the message."

"Bien sur, they will get it from several angles. That will be a concern but not a problem—until after we spring our surprise."

"Possibly, but of course knowing what they plan is key to the whole proceeding. That does concern me greatly. I don't suppose you all have any useful assets on the ground."

Deby offered a reassuring nod. "We might be able to look under a few stones and see what we can find."

"If nothing else, we can see what they come across the border with, surely."

"Perhaps better than that."

The major appeared pleased. "Appreciated and vital."

Martin admired the major's touch. He seemed to know just how far to push things.

"Colonel, if I might, another rather large question mark is refueling the plane. Can you get a tanker truck to the strip? The terrain is bound to be rugged."

"Correct, but we have used it before. The track is passable, if not comfortable."

"Okay then. Next item. The colonel is bound to send a large detachment to guard such a valuable resource as Tinner."

"Probably, but we will be prepared for that. We will have enough men that they won't think of resisting."

"Which begs the next question: What will we do with them once we have Tinner?"

"That is easy, Major. Colonel Ghaddafi has many of our people in his prisons. We will be glad to trade."

"That, of course, won't include Herr Professor Tinner."

Martin loved how the major gift-wrapped statements in questions. "Or Russell and the Cubans," Martin added.

"I know some people who will be anxious to talk to them," the major said, "though they may not be saying much after Mobutu's lads finish with them."

Martin was beginning to feel a bit better about the plan, but questions remained. "Okay," he said, "so you all know where I'm going to be. Personally, I'm pretty interested in where you all will be. What's the general non-Martin part of the plan?"

The major pumped his eyebrows. "Just what we are here for, old boy. So, Etienne and Colonel, I presume you all have had some discussions about this."

Deby stepped forward. "Of course, and I think that we have come up with a good plan." He looked over at Etienne, who nodded. "Major, our plan is to take them at a location we have selected about a mile from the strip. Then we will put our chaps in their uniforms and come meet you as arranged. We will have a gun on Tinner and anyone else who is important."

"You're one hundred percent confident that you won't give them a chance to alert Agent Russell? Remember: our friend here will have no cover. I have no doubt who Russell will shoot first if he has any suspicions."

Deby smiled. "Without going into unnecessary detail, Major, I can assure you that we will know exactly who does what on the Libyan side of things."

"Comforting to hear, but I wasn't really expecting any less."

Another question dawned on Martin. "Major, where are you planning to be? Obviously, not with me."

"Up here awaiting your arrival with bated breath. I'm quite sure Etienne will be with me, as I suspect he may wish to handle Agent Russell personally."

"You're a hundred percent sure Russell will be along for the ride?"

"Of course. This is a one-way trip for him—has to be. His keepers will never forgive him for this, whether they think he was involved or not. The only way he goes back to Langley is in cuffs."

"Okay, now for the tough one, at least for me." Martin took a deep breath. "What happens to me in his book?"

"You're asking if he plans on killing you? Bloody obvious. Of course he does. But not until the deal is done. Then that letter won't matter. We'll take care of that possibility when you land, but in the meantime, you'll be armed."

"So will he and the Cubans, and I can't see them letting me stay armed."

"Too true. That's why we'll be leaving several backups in convenient places on the Antonov. Equally, Lucienne is proficient and knows he won't be making the return trip if we don't take care of business."

Martin wished he shared the major's confidence. "It's going to be a long plane ride, with the cat watching the mice watch the cat."

"Builds character, old boy." The major's tone said save it for later. "In any event, we still have much to work out—and only a few days to do so. Etienne, how are things progressing on your end?"

Etienne appeared eager to close out the conversation. "Progressing, nicely. Monsieur le President has had several fruitful conversations with President Tombalbaye." He glanced at Deby, who nodded. "It seems he can benefit at this time from some American generosity. Can't we all?"

"Quite, and I can assure you that they'll be generous—after the fact. We, of course, cannot let anything slip to them until after the fact."

Etienne rose. "Gentlemen, is there anything else right now? If not, I suggest we meet the same time and place in three days."

As the others started for the door, the major signaled Martin to stay. "Hang about a bit. There are a few things that I need to go over with you. They don't concern the others."

Martin was grateful for the one-on-one. "I was kind of wondering when we were going to sit down and hash some things out."

"Things moved fast. I appreciate your patience. The game's afoot, and the stakes are pretty high this time around."

"To quote you, *quite*. Nukes for the mad colonel. The mind boggles. So, Major, assuming this is unofficial, just how did you stumble across it, and why not let the adults handle it?"

"Your mother didn't raise a stupid firstborn. The tale starts and ends with your good friend Agent Russell. Oddly enough, and in a funny way, it does tie back to the Shaba diamonds. I was chatting to Russell, convincing him that there was no reason to kill you, when I mentioned that the cousins should be more worried about uranium and cobalt smuggling than a few diamonds."

Martin leaned forward, unable to hide the look of his surprise on his face. "One of the few times you ever said too much."

"You know how to kick a man when he's down."

"That's the first opportunity you've ever given me. So how did you get wind of it?"

"Friends in the wrong places."

"But of course. So . . . what's in all of this for you? And I expect a less professional answer, if you know what I mean."

"Quite. You do have a pound of flesh in this. The more appropriate question is what's in this for both of us? I mean, the big prize is getting rid of that scum Agent Russell, but I'm half of a mind to retire soon."

Martin tried not to laugh. "Really. That I can't quite see. What the hell are you going to do with yourself?"

"Well, old boy, I have a hankering to find myself a nice place on the beach. Maybe do a bit of freelance work—obviously for the good guys. I've built up enough contacts over the years. There wouldn't be any shortage of business. Most importantly, I could pick and choose."

"No doubt about the business end of that. Surely there will be bonuses or whatever for all of us."

"Of course, maybe even a bit of your record expunged by our friends in Langley."

"That's a thought. I'm sure Russell didn't paint a pretty picture."

"You're not a well-thought-of chap right now, but this will go a long way to change that. Assuming we pull this off. What are *your* plans?"

Martin sighed. Imagining the future felt like a fool's errand. "I don't know, to be honest. I haven't given it a great deal of thought. Actually, I haven't given anything much thought."

"It might not be that bad a time to do that. I know Mapende was a rum blow. I lost someone early on too. It was my fault. She was a double I'd fallen in love with out of Syria. She'd been compromised when we were running an exfil to Beirut. She wanted to go the night before. There was no evidence that the operation was blown, so I said no."

"And she was killed?"

"Yes, and I will never get over it—just *past* it, as they say."

"That's why no marriage?"

"Yes, never trusted myself to commit to a woman after that. Now I regret that. There have been women here and there, but I could never let myself go with my heart."

"Funny, I haven't been attracted to any woman since Mapende—not until Chlothilde."

"She's a good one, but perhaps not right for you right now. Trust me. True love will occur again. You're young. In the meantime, not wanting to butt in, but you need to start a career or something to keep you occupied. I know you have some money, but—"

"You're right. Think I'm going to get back to serious writing."

"Why not? You've got a nose for intel and know how to intentionally network. Taught by the best, if I might add. I always told you our endeavors were basically the same. We just get paid by a different boss. That said, you've got the material for a couple of good novels now."

"Okay, so truth or dare time. I'm a little concerned about how things are going to play out. We're flying pretty blind here."

"Can't disagree on that one. Always that way on a deal like this one. Comes down to our partners, doesn't it? No problems with Etienne. Trust him with my life and have in the past. We'll just have to take his word on the Chadian chap."

"The problem is that it's the big unknown piece. You're way smarter and more experienced than I am. I haven't been able to come up with any way we can manage that risk better. What happens if we have plane problems?"

"That one isn't that hard. Our Chadian buddies will just have to help us out. I'm sure that Tombalbaye has cut himself a good deal with Mobutu, but not knowing Mobutu, it will be contingent on Monsieur le President getting back his goods and Agent Russell to boot. The bigger problem will be if Frolinat shows up—or the Libyans in big numbers."

"Again, on the Chadians, for sure. So why aren't we thinking about ambushing them before they can get the drop on us?"

"Exactly, old boy. You're learning. That's what Etienne and I are scheming up right now. The plan within the plan would be to ambush them as they come into the strip. Our Chadian friend has a source in Tripoli. He figures to know their route and the disposition of their forces. We bag them early, change uniforms to fool Agent Russell and crew, and come to the strip."

"Sounds simple. It won't be."

"Too right. Timmer is a prized asset. They'll have the A team guarding him. Still, it won't be a big force. This one will be a smash-and-grab in their books. Remember: They aren't expecting resistance. They don't know their opp has been burned."

"What about Russell doing the same to me at the Kinshasa end?"

"He won't do that, old boy. *Can't*, actually. Remember: He's still hoping to pull this off and pin it on some Cuban mercenaries working for Gaddafi. He collects the Libyan loot, goes back to Langley, and lives happily ever after. He can't be leaving bodies about in Kinshasa and having to explain. No, he'll be planning to dispose of you and the Cubans at the rendezvous in the strip. In his mind, he'll have overwhelming force on hand and plenty of desert to bury you in."

Martin frowned grimly as he imagined what Russell had in store for him. "You're right about that."

"My guess is he'll tell the Libyans to kill you and the Cubans once the plane is unloaded."

"That should leave plenty of time, but I want a gun or two stashed around the plane. I don't plan on getting off unarmed."

"You'd better not. Plus, we'll have a code on radio coms prior to your landing letting you know everything is ready. Otherwise, you and the pilot will have to wing it—no pun intended."

Martin ignored the bad joke. "I assume the plan is to take them all prisoner and fly them back to Kinshasa."

"All except the Libyans. We'll leave them to Deby and the Chadians. I'm sure they'll find something useful to do with them. Hostage swap, methinks."

"You always make it sound so easy."

"It is, old boy, until the first shot is fired and everything goes pear-shaped. The good news is that you know how to handle yourself. Otherwise, you wouldn't be here."

CHAPTER

22

MARTIN WAS ALONE with his thoughts on the ride back to the hotel. It was definitely getting real in a hurry. He noticed the flat, coppery taste of adrenalin and felt its pull once again. Fuck, he loved it. *Damm the torpedoes.* He consciously downshifted as they entered the center of town. It was getting real, and he had some serious thinking to do.

"*Mon dieu, qu'est ce qui arrive.*" Hippolyte's tone snapped Martin from his reverie.

A large boisterous crowd was milling around in front of the hotel. Just as Martin and Hippolyte neared the hotel, a large white Land Rover pulled up in front, and Ali and entourage got out.

"Park across the street," Martin said. "I don't want to miss this. None of this is an accident. Ali is going to put on a show. You should never miss an Ali show."

"Bien sur, he does seem to like them."

"Part of the package."

Ali got out of the limo and started shadow-boxing, whipping the crowd into a frenzy with some of his patented shuffles.

"Ali Bombaye! Ali kill him!" The crowd heaved and stomped. The police could hardly contain them.

Ali fed off their energy. "Where's that ugly George? He's so ugly his mother had to pull the sheet up over his head so sleep could sneak up on him!"

Suddenly Martin realized what was going on. Ali was mobilizing the crowd, building their energy to siphon it off for the epic confrontation to come. From what Martin had seen of Foreman, Ali would need every bit of it.

Martin slipped around the edge of the crowd and through the deserted lobby to his room.

The quiet was bliss. From his balcony, he looked down at the melee on the street and saw that it hadn't abated in the slightest. Don King and his gold lamé suit and Brillo-pad hairdo emerged from the hotel and gave Ali a rapturous hug. Cue pandemonium.

Russell was right about one thing, Martin thought: The fight made for the perfect cover for the opp.

Chlothilde had invited him to dinner that night at her father's. Martin was looking forward to reading the room. The major was the major. Martin loved him. But when his blood was up, it was *up*. It was always nice to triangulate things with the locals.

...

Chlothilde met Martin at the door. "So good to see you. Etienne is here too."

"Is that a heads-up, a warning, or gossip?"

"Mechant." She caressed his cheek. "Possibly all three."

It was just the four of them. Martin wondered what was going on. Perhaps nothing, but his antennae were definitely tuned in.

"Bienvenue, Martin," Henri said. "What can I get you?"

"A beer would be fine. Thanks." Martin turned to Etienne. "Nice to see you here. I hope it isn't all business."

"*Pas de tout*, but certainly we will talk a little. After all, it's only a week to the big night. I am interested to hear how you feel about things."

Martin chuckled. "That makes two of us. Who goes first?"

Etienne toasted Martin's bottle. "You, of course. You just spent time with the major and others pulling things together. Monsieur le President is very interested in this matter. Its outcome could affect many important relationships."

"True enough. As far as I'm concerned, things seem to be shaping up okay. That said, like all of these types of deals, as I'm sure you're aware, the plan only lasts until the first shot is fired."

"Perhaps there won't be any shots fired."

"Nice thought—dream. I somehow don't think so. I don't believe that you do, either."

"Touche. Yes, there are going to be too many groups with too many guns with too much at stake to make it likely that things will go off without a hitch."

"Russell scares me. He's unpredictable. Plus, he's got options, which complicates things."

"Options?"

"Sure. Let's say he smells a rat when we land in the zone. He has the option of offing me and the major and anyone else who interferes and just heading over the border. Not his preferred scenario, but viable. We don't have a bailout if things go wrong."

"Mais non, perhaps not one you have thought of."

"True enough. I would've thought the major would have at least two bailout scenarios. He thinks very highly of you, too, Etienne, so what gives?"

"Let's start at the beginning. Russell needs you, the pilot, and the plane to get up to the zone, so that part is okay. We will, of course, have hidden several weapons for you and the pilot. Russell will undoubtedly search and disarm you prior to taking off."

"That follows, and he has to leave things clean in Kinshasa for his story to hold up. My concern has always been the other end in the Aouzou Strip. From what I hear, it's pretty much no man's land up there."

Etienne nodded. "Much of the time you are correct, but we can and will project force up there with the aid of Colonel Deby. He is able, and we have worked together successfully before. Most importantly, our respective bosses are very interested in this matter concluding successfully."

"I assume that you've made alternate arrangements in case the plane gets damaged in the crossfire, for instance."

"Bien sure. Extra trucks, an alternative strip, with a plane fueled and ready laid on."

"Sounds like enough to get me into dinner."

Henri and Chlothilde deftly shifted the conversation to other topics during the dinner, which suited Martin. He needed some mental time off. As the big day drew closer, it was growing increasingly hard to find much respite. Much as he loved adrenalin, it was a drain.

• • •

Chlothilde did her best to distract Martin when they got back to her house. She was only partially successful. "Cheri, you are not all here."

"Sorry, you're right. Part of me is up in the Aouzou Strip. The part of me that's here is worried about many things."

"Such as, cheri? Are you tired of me already?"

"Nope," Martin said, shaking his head. "That's the problem. I'm getting fonder of you by the minute."

"So?"

"Things didn't work out too well the last time that happened."

"Yes, the major told me about that. It is sad, no?"

"Yes, I wouldn't want it to happen again, if things went somehow wrong."

"Martin, I am fond of you—fonder all the time. I don't know what that means for either of us in the long term." She kissed him. "I think we must wait until this is over. I don't see any way that I am involved, so I should be okay."

"I hope so, but you're Henri's daughter. Kinshasa is small. Your father is a big fish. Russell is crazy enough to do anything if he gets desperate."

"Yes, that is true. I don't like being in the same room as him." She shuddered. "He doesn't care about anything but himself. A true psychopath."

"I would presume your father and Etienne have thought carefully about all of the possible scenarios."

"Of course, and the major." She fixed him with her gaze. "But everything changes when the game starts."

CHAPTER

23

MARTIN HEADED DOWN early for breakfast. The only good thing about the influx of the fight crowd was that they tended to stay up late partying, which made for a quiet dining room come breakfast time. Or so he thought.

"How's my favorite Yank entrepreneur?" Russell looked crisp in khakis and a madras sports jacket.

"You do know how to ruin a guy's breakfast. Why are you looking so dapper this morning?"

"I might be meeting some important folks—you never know. Speaking of which, Chlothilde is a very lovely woman. You seem to like her company, and who can blame you? She's very well-connected."

"And?"

Fuck him, Martin thought. No one had ever accused the bastard of being subtle, but then again, subtlety was not required for intimidation, which was Russell's strong suit—as well as his penchant for violence.

"It would be a shame if she were somehow to become caught up in this."

"You know, Russell, I can't figure out your compulsive need

163

to be so obvious. Do you think it's more intimidating, makes you look smarter—what?"

Russell offered a nonchalant shrug. "Just saying."

"Okay, so you didn't come here just to lean on me a little. What gives?"

"Oh, I don't know. A little birdy told me that your old buddy might be in town."

"Who's that?"

Russell drew back in dismay. "Please."

"The major, you mean."

"You two are usually joined at the hip. If he's around, that might make a man nervous."

"That's on you. I came over here to look into other opportunities. Then you just happened to pop up—not so coincidentally, it seems to me. Anyway, your play isn't really his sort of thing, is it?"

"Stopping it might be."

"This is a little outside of his normal playpen, though."

"This same little birdie told me that he goes back a ways with Mobutu. Back to the early days. Tshombe and all that."

Martin tried to play dumb. "He never told me about that, so I can't help you there. Besides, from what I hear, you guys should know all about that."

"Don't know much about that. It was before my time."

One good lie deserved another, Martin thought. "Somehow I think you have enough assets around town that you'll know he's here before I do."

Russell let that one pass. "We're getting close. Only a few days until the big event, no pun intended. Do be careful to keep me in the loop about anything I should know."

"Of course. Remember: My ass is on the line too."

Martin gave Russell ten minutes and slipped out the rear entrance of the hotel to his and Hippolyte's carefully chosen spot.

The major had given him a basic course in surveillance detection and evasion back in Uganda. "It can sometimes be a bit counterintuitive, old boy. For instance, no trained observer is going to park on a parallel street to his or her quarry—too easy to spot. They'll be trained to park on the closest horizontal street where they can still see the egress. So have your driver park in the same place. They'll know, and so will you."

Words to live by.

Martin surveyed the street. No tails in sight. In fact, no vehicle except Hippolyte's. He was napping.

Martin tapped lightly on the window. "Bonjour, mon ami. You need to talk to Etienne immediately. We'll need to meet as soon as possible. The major too. We have a problem."

"D'accord. I will go make a call. Take a walk around for five minutes and come back."

Martin took a leisurely stroll. Kinshasa was just waking up. He could feel the electricity. The fight was by far the biggest thing that had ever happened there. Even the beggars were panhandling with more energy than normal. Good on them, Martin thought. This was their chance to prey on all that white guilt.

● ● ●

Hippolyte had the engine running. "Allez-y, they want to see you *a l'instant.*"

They set off and soon entered a part of town that Martin had never been to. He noticed that there were no whites around. The buildings were ramshackle and old. They pulled up in front of an electrical parts store. It was better stocked than the others, with new-looking equipment stacked neatly on metal shelves, and the several Surete types loitering nearby looked alert. Something was up.

As Martin stepped inside the shop, Etienne stuck his head out of the back-office door and waved him inside.

The major handed him a frosty beer and gestured him to a seat. "Okay, let's have it."

"So our mutual friend has, as you know, gotten in the habit of ruining my breakfasts. True to form, he popped in this morning, and it wasn't about the fight—ha ha. He started by telling me what good taste I had in woman, what a catch Chlothilde was, so well-connected, blah, blah, blah, spreading it on thick. Then he got to the real point. He told me that a little birdie had told him that the major was in town."

"Hmm . . ." The major let that hang for a while before looking over at Etienne. "Eh bien?"

"There could be many explanations," Etienne replied.

"Absolutely, old man. That wasn't about blame as much as it was to understand if and how it changes things."

"Well," Martin said, "it's stating the obvious, but you have to proceed as if he knows for a fact you're here. I tried to throw him off with, 'It's not your normal hunting ground,' and all that stuff. He wasn't having any. Said you knew Mobutu from the Tshombe days."

"He's a little young to have been around then, but word does get around."

"Unsubtle as it was, I don't much like the Chlothilde inference, either."

"We'll have to think things through clearly. Etienne, is there any chance there's a leak in your shoppe?"

Etienne pursed his lips as he thought over the question. "Anything is possible, but I find it unlikely. We have kept this in a very tight circle for obvious reasons. Of course, enquiries—serious—will be made."

Martin eyed the major. "Not sure what you being underfoot

adds to Russell's thinking besides general been-there-seen-that-done-that paranoia."

"Lots, old boy. The expected is hard enough to deal with. No one worth their salt wants jokers in the pack. He'll be very anxious to figure out why I've suddenly surfaced. It could be a good opportunity to plant a little misinformation, eh, Etienne?"

Etienne laughed. "How did I guess that was where you'd be going?"

"Because the student has passed the teacher. Is there much going on in Shaba these days?"

"I hesitate to say this, but it is rather quiet at the moment. However, several of the mining contracts are coming up for renegotiation, especially Okimo. No doubt Agent Russell is aware of your role in the original disposition of those assets."

"Yes, I'm sure that you can get your boss to leak some interesting tidbits. Maybe we use that chap Nimi he seems to be so fond of."

"As always, Major, you have a good idea. Nimi is perfect for Russell. They are so similar—and dangerous for the same reasons."

"Quite. But subtlety is neither's strong suit. Why not say that the president wants to shake up the bidding for the operating contracts and might want to bring in some British mining interests? Anglo American could be whispered."

"Certainement. That would explain your presence—at least adequately for Russell."

"So let's get that in the works ASAP." The major was in his element and warming to the task." Okay, Etienne, how are things going with our friends up north?"

"On schedule. The Chadeans will have a carefully chosen battalion of their elite special forces plus assorted armor and other assets. There will be plenty enough to handle anything the colonel or Frolinat bring to the party."

"I don't have to ask if they'll have eyes on them the minute they cross the border. No surprises then. This is big-boy stuff."

"Agreed," Etienne said. "There are a couple of things that we should consider, though. What is our backup if the plane gets damaged in a firefight?"

"Yes, I was wondering when you'd get to that. I assume we can truck everyone down to another strip and borrow a plane from the Chadians. Obviously, we'll need to negotiate that in advance."

"I already started the discussion with Colonel Deby. It will not be a problem. I believe those arrangements have already been negotiated at a far higher level."

"Quite. Still, I'd like to run an eye over them, if at all possible."

"D'accord. I will get them to you tomorrow."

The major seemed satisfied as he turned to Martin. "Any questions?"

"Tons, but probably not many that you can answer."

"Well, look at the bright side, old boy: There's a lot more to do in Kinshasa than the Seses, and there's always Chlothilde."

"That's part of the problem."

The major stroked his chin. "Hmm . . . I see where you're going. Shouldn't happen this time. She won't be directly involved like Mapende was."

"Yeah, I wasn't worried until that asshole mentioned her."

"I wouldn't be too concerned about that. It's pretty standard playbook stuff. Grooming the battlefield with a little intimidation is a favorite of his sort. Still, there's history, so we must take it seriously. Etienne, are you aware of the history?"

"Yes," Etienne said, nodding, "I read the dossier. Unfortunate, Martin. We will definitely provide adequate security. Chlothilde's father is a trusted confidante of the president."

Martin knew that was as much as he could expect. "So what's the plan for the night of the event? I'm still worried about Russell throwing me out of the plane at ten thousand feet."

The major was slow to respond. "Yes, been giving that some thought."

"That's encouraging. So?"

"I'm thinking, old cock."

"That's what I'm afraid of."

Etienne laughed and slapped the table. "I have it. Russell *does* have a weakness. She is named Sarah."

The major's eyes widened in surprise. "Really? That snake actually cares about someone besides himself?"

"Truly. He requested permission to marry her a few weeks ago."

"I knew you all were good," the major said in an admiring tone, "but not *that* good. I'm impressed."

"It's not that hard, Major. We have ears in many places. That kind of information is not that closely guarded. The cable asking for it wasn't even coded."

"So," the major replied, "what do you know about this Sarah?"

"She works for the commercial attaché. She's been in post for about eighteen months. It's a simple matter. We know where she lives."

"So we snatch her the night of the event, and Martin is untouchable in return for her safety. Easily done, old bean, but we'll have to keep it on the QT. The cousins won't be best pleased."

"Not half as displeased as they will be when they find out what Russell was really up to. I suspect any side action will get lost in the fracas, so to speak." Etienne nodded to Martin. "Monsieur Fine, any comments?"

Martin exhaled slowly. "Well, I feel a lot better than I did ten minutes ago—assuming it all goes to plan."

"It is the least complicated piece of the business."

"Agreed," the major said, " but we'll want some of your best men on it."

"Bien sur, I have the right men all set."

The major's eyes danced. "Well, that seems to be as far as we can go right now. I assume, Etienne, that you're locking down all of the details as we speak. Seven days till the balloon drops. Let's go about our business as boringly as possible. I suggest we rendezvous again in three or four days at another of Etienne's safehouses."

• • •

During the drive back to the hotel, Martin was too lost in his thoughts to absorb the urban landscape streaming by outside the passenger window. The closer they got to the date, the flimsier their plans—if he could call them that—seemed. He exhaled. Anything more concrete wouldn't last past the first shot. Bad analogy, he thought.

The receptionist flagged him at the hotel and handed him a note from Chlothilde.

> *We are invited to Father's country house on the river for the weekend. I will meet you at the hotel in two hours.*

Okay with me, he thought. It sure beat hanging around with his own adrenalin-fueled angst.

He showered, shoved a few clothes in the bag, and went down to the bar to have a beer while he waited.

Russell showed up a few minutes later, making his second appearance of the day. "How'd I know I'd find you here, Fine?"

"I have to stop drinking here," Martin said. "Too easy to find."

"Don't kid yourself. I always know where to find you."

"Okay, so you proved that. To what do I owe this singular pleasure? Haven't we seen enough of each other already today?"

"Like I said earlier, things are getting close. Just checking that everything is in order on your side. No surprises. They wouldn't be welcome at this point."

"That might be one of the few things we can agree on."

"You going someplace?" Russell nudged his bag with his toe. "Say hi to Chlothilde and Henri for me."

Martin was surprised—but knew he shouldn't be. How much did the man know? Did they have a mole in their camp? "I will. I'm sure it'll make their weekend."

If Russell got the sarcasm, it didn't register. Martin hoped he wasn't as bulletproof as he thought he was. The man was indeed keeping close tabs on him—a disquieting thought.

Russell slinked off, and before Martin could indulge his apprehensions further, Chlothilde arrived.

She kissed him. "Cheri, you have that look again."

"Russell just walked on my grave. Second time today. I feel like I should shower every time I meet him. So. What's on for the weekend? I hear some of the spots up the river are scenic. I'm sure your father's is special."

"Let's go. You will like it."

The ride out was interesting once they cleared the sprawl of Kinshasa. The country was surprisingly open and less like the tropical rain forest that enveloped most of Zaire. Unfortunately, the traffic was still dense with trucks and camions—the minibuses that buzzed about overloaded to the gills and belching toxic fumes.

"So who's going to be at this little soiree?"

"Not sure. Papa was vague as he sometimes can be—usually when someone really important might be coming."

"Monsieur le President, perhaps?"

"I really don't know. Does it matter?" She glared out the window. "This traffic is horrible."

As if to confirm her point, Hippolyte swerved violently to miss a camion that pulled out in front of them with no warning.

Mon dieu, Martin thought. It might as well have been New York on a summer Friday. They certainly weren't the only folks getting out of Kinshasa for the weekend.

Martin let his thoughts roam. Things were moving fast. It was hard to keep up with the rapidly shifting landscape. There wasn't time to think about all of the things they were doing wrong. What had started out as a little piece of revenge had morphed into cobalt smuggling with a dose of kidnapping and God-knew-what-else.

"Martin, you are somewhere else."

"I was having dangerous thoughts—to the tune of, 'How did I get myself into this?'"

"A little late, cheri."

"Touche. Of course you're right, but I sometimes think that if I at least ask the question, I'm not as crazy as I sometimes think I am."

"Do you really want me to answer that?"

"Nope. Not going there, and neither should you."

"It all goes back to Mapende, right?"

"How do you know her name?"

"The major told us all about the Affaire Aka. Maybe you are not over her."

"Or maybe I'm worried the same thing will happen to you, because I've grown very fond of you."

"That hadn't escaped me, and I of you. It is not an easy situation. I certainly didn't plan on meeting or becoming fond of an American adventurer."

"Is that what I am? An adventurer?"

"Bien sur. What would you call yourself?"

"Never thought about it before. You sure know how to ruin a party." It occurred to Martin that he hadn't thought about much since that day on Lamu. "Sorry, you're right. And it hurts. It hurts because I care about you, and I should be thinking about lots of things besides myself and my petty need for revenge."

They drove on in silence for a while. What was there to say? It was like he had awakened from an eighteen-month-long nightmare. Everything—all his senses—seemed to have awakened. The bad news was that he wasn't necessarily liking what he was seeing with his new set of eyes.

"You went quiet again," she said. "What is it?"

"Thinking suddenly about things I should have been thinking about for a while now."

"Really, you can't have been asleep this whole time. *Non ce n'est pas possible.*"

"Not asleep, for sure, but not totally awake either. Not with respect to you. Looking at you, I realize that I really am fond of you. Having someone I don't want to lose woke me up."

"I am so glad to hear you say that. I hoped it, as I have strong feelings for you too."

Martin suddenly felt relieved, like a weight had been lifted. But on the other hand, he was still suffering the Esther hangover. It couldn't happen twice, could it? He wasn't entirely happy the fog he'd been walking around in had suddenly dissolved. He felt something he hadn't felt in a while—fear.

The rest of the drive passed in silence until Hippolyte turned into a driveway lined with flamboyant orange-blossomed trees.

"Always loved these trees," Martin said. "They're so orange they look phony."

"Father planted them when I was very young, so I have grown up with them."

"Sure is peaceful after Kinshasa."

The driveway curved around a large cluster of rocks, and the house, which was set well back from the limpid brown river, came into sight.

"A swim looks tempting," Martin said, "but I don't even want to guess what's lurking in there."

"Lots of crocodiles and other nasty things. That is why we have a pool and a strong fence by the water."

The bungalow was large with screened-in, wrap-around verandahs and lazy overhead fans barely moving the air.

The houseman emerged and gave Chlothilde a half bow. "Madame Chlothilde, your father called. He won't be coming until later this evening."

Chlothilde gave him a hug. "Mustafa, meet my good friend Martin. You don't have to be formal with him."

Mustafa was short and wore a leopard-skin sash around his crisp beige tunic. He smiled and ushered them in with a bow.

Martin looked around with envy. It was like a Hollywood set for an African hunting lodge. Stuffed animal heads, intermixed with old, funky masks, hung from the walls. Zebra skins covered the wooden floors.

"Somehow, it's what I expected." Martin wandered the great room, taking it in. "Love the masks."

"Those are father's pride and joy. The animals were here when he brought it. I am glad hunting is not his thing."

A car pulled up.

Chlothilde glanced out the window. "There are our other surprise guests." She smiled. "I think you have met them before."

Martin looked out the door and laughed. "I should've known. What a surprise: the major and Etienne, the perfect pair to round out the weekend."

The major chuckled in return. "Well, old cock, nice spot for the weekend. Good timing too. Game's afoot, for sure. Etienne and I thought this was the perfect time for a final run-through of the plans."

"Bien sur," Etienne said, nodding, "we have precious little time until we start things."

"Aren't you all traveling a little light?" Martin asked. "I don't see any security detail—not like you two."

"Patience, lad." The major pointed out the window.

A Land Rover pulled up, and two obvious security types got out and started pacing the perimeter of the compound.

"Never leave home without them."

"What about the others?" Martin gestured out the window as a much more battered pickup fishtailed to a halt outside.

Five heavily armed men jumped out.

Etienne's two guards didn't hesitate and opened fire, taking down one of them, but the others cut them down with a burst of AK fire.

In the bungalow, Martin and the others dove for cover. The major and Etienne drew pistols and turned over the couches and crawled behind them, signaling Chlothilde and Martin to do the same.

The major fired some warning shots out the window and ducked behind a couch. "Four of the buggers left as far as I can make out."

Another burst from outside shattered the windows.

"We can't just sit here, or they'll have us. They're not short of bloody ammo."

Mustafa crawled out from the back with an AK, which he slid across the floor to the major.

The major fired off two bursts in the direction of the men outside. He slid his pistol over to Martin. "You have five rounds left. Guard Chlothilde. Etienne and I will try to flank them." He scrambled back toward the kitchen while Etienne fired more covering rounds outside.

The guys outside were indiscriminately riddling the house.

Martin covered Chlothilde with his body as the rounds shredded the upholstery above them. "Fuck, Major, this isn't looking good!"

"No choice for it. We're going to have to move out of here, or they'll get us. You and Chlothilde start crawling to the back. Follow Mustafa very carefully." He loosed off a few more rounds in the direction of the attackers.

Just as Martin and Chlothilde started to crawl toward the rear, a burst of bullets caught Mustafa across the chest. He coughed up blood and went limp.

Martin fired two shots through the door to the hall where the fire had come from as he and Chlothilde scrambled back to the cover behind the couch. They were fucked. He covered Chlothilde again and said his prayers.

The major looked grim as he fired off economical bursts. "Etienne, how many do you have left?'

"Only three, mon vieux." Another burst from outside splintered the floorboards between them. "Merde, they are closing in."

Just then, the fire stopped from outside, followed by a hail of automatic fire from the front and the back of the house. It sounded like several additional gunmen or more. Then silence.

Martin traded glances with the major and waited.

The major signaled them not to move. "I think it's good news, but wondering who it could be."

Three heavily armed soldiers entered. Martin, following the major's cues, dropped his weapon and raised his hands.

Shortly after, Mobutu stepped inside.

"Your Excellency," the major gushed, "are we glad to see you!"

"Likewise, Major. Etienne, Chlothilde. So…" Mobutu paused for effect, then headed over to the well-stocked bar and poured himself a stiff scotch, gesturing the others to do so. "The men outside are Cuban—at least that's what their ID says. As I recall, our obnoxious Ami friend likes to use Cubans for his dirty work. Do tell, Etienne, how this escaped your attention."

"Monsieur le President, I do not know."

"That's not good enough, and you know it."

The tension in the room was palpable. Mobutu waived the troops out with a contemptuous flick of his wrist. "And while we are asking questions that should not have to be asked, who were they after? Surely not our American friend. Agent Russell needs him."

"That's true, Monsieur le President." The major took a deep swig and rolled it around his tongue appreciatively. "Always tastes better after a bit of drama. I reckon it had to be me and Etienne. After all, in his eyes, we're the main barriers to the successful completion of the plan."

Mobutu savored a sip. "That does make sense. I am presuming that he wanted it to happen in front of Mr. Fine, *pour encourager les autres*."

"Quite. That would be the unsubtle Agent Russell thing to do."

"D'accord. We are agreed on that point, which brings us to the important part of this discussion. How do we turn all of this to our advantage?"

"That one is simple, Your Excellency." The major finished his scotch. "We let him think he succeeded."

Mobutu got up, stretched, and refreshed his drink. "I think so. A nice big funeral for you, Etienne. Lots of visibility. Who knows? I might even be persuaded to attend. Sadly, Major, something far more discreet for you, but we will make sure that Mr. Russell is aware."

Etienne walked outside and started barking orders. "I will get the right journalists out here to cover our demise. Major, you and I will have to make ourselves absent for a few days."

Mobutu paused briefly as he walked past. "You two disappear for three days. I will see to the funerals and all the details. Mr. Fine, you and Chlothilde will remain here, suitably shaken, until Henri arrives. No one besides us is to know Etienne and the major survived. I will leave the guards. They are my personal detail. They will say nothing." He waved them back inside and barked a series of orders.

The major and Etienne drove off for parts unknown.

"Well," Martin said, taking Chlothilde by the hand, "that was a non-relaxing way to start a relaxing weekend."

"It's not funny!" she hissed.

"Yep, it's a serious reminder of the fact that this is big-boy stuff. Not that I really needed any reminding."

"Aren't you scared?"

"Sometimes. *Most* times. But I love the rush, the adrenalin. Can't say why, but there's nothing like it."

"You are crazy," she said, shaking her head as she studied his face.

"Definitely one of life's great ironies that you never feel more alive than when you're about to die."

A car door slammed outside.

She seemed to stiffen and then nodded past the shattered glass. "Here comes Father. What are we going to tell him?"

"Exactly what we were told to," Martin said. "Not a word more or less."

Henri gestured at Mobutu's security detail and then eyed the mess. "Mon Dieu, what has happened here?"

"Oh, Papa, horrible things." Chlothilde collapsed into Henri's arms sobbing. It was an Oscar-worthy performance, and Martin was impressed. "It was horrible. Etienne and the major were assassinated."

"Mon Dieux, by who?"

"Russell's Cubans."

Henri walked over to the bar and poured himself a large scotch. "The man is a sociopath. He must pay for this."

"He will, Papa. The president was here just after you saw his guards."

Henri turned to Martin. "Were they after you too?"

"I doubt it, but there are lots of questions running through my head. As for me, unlikely I was the target, since I was setting up the flights to get the stuff out. For now, I'm guessing it was opportunistic that they were tailing them and decided this was a nice, secluded spot to do it."

Henri passed out scotches. "Still, it is lucky that you are standing here in front of me. The major—it is hard for me to believe that he is gone. Etienne too. And killed in my house! It is hard to comprehend."

"It is a mind-full," Martin said, "but it's also a serious warning. I can't countenance life without the major, especially to get through the rest of this, but the best revenge will be to finish the deal and bury these bastards."

Henri frowned. "Yes, you are right."

Chlothilde choked back a sob. "I don't want to stay here tonight."

Henri finished his scotch. "None of us will stay, but we must make sure that we have good security. We still don't know what Agent Russell was really up to."

"True," Martin said, "and I can't see the president moving on him without the proverbial smoking gun. I think I'll be all right as long as he still thinks he needs me."

"You are probably right, but the same might not apply to Chlothilde and I. I will call the president to arrange more men. I am sure it will be in place by the time you get home."

It wasn't comfortable at the bungalow with all that had happened.

Henri made a few calls and headed for the door with one of Mobutu's guards. On the way out, he kissed Chlothilde. "Don't worry. The president is giving you the other guard. We will make more permanent arrangements tomorrow. For now, be alert.

Martin, I suggest you stay with Chlothilde tonight until we can make more organized arrangements."

"Are you sure that's wise?" Martin asked. "Just thinking that if Russell's guys were only after the major and Etienne, we don't want to tip our hand that they didn't succeed by suddenly guarding me too."

"You are right, Martin, but I am worried about Chlothilde."

"Fair enough." There was no point in arguing, Martin thought. Besides, Henri didn't know that the major and Etienne were okay.

It was a quiet drive back to Kinshasa. Martin was processing. Everything that had seemed dreamlike before—African surreal, as he liked to think of it—now seemed clear, sharp, and not a little menacing. Nothing like a couple of shootings to focus a man.

• • •

"Martin, it didn't seem real until now." Chlothilde paced in the living room, restlessly playing with her worry beads.

"My thoughts exactly, but now it's as real as it gets. Let's stay cool and think. I'm sure the major will come up with a good plan."

"I believe so, but Papa will be worried."

"As he should be. But I assume the president will give you security."

"And in the meantime?"

"We act as if everything is abnormally normal, meaning we mourn the major and Etienne publicly and wait for them to be back in touch privately, as I am sure they will be."

Neither of them had much to say after that. Shock was replaced by numbness. Martin felt drained as he tried to work his way through the suddenly rearranged pieces of the puzzle. Chlothilde didn't protest when he said he was going back to the hotel after dropping her at her house, where the extra security was visibly in place.

"Let's talk in the morning. Things will be clearer then," he said with more confidence than he felt as he kissed her goodbye.

• • •

The next two days passed slowly. Martin wasn't sure what to do with himself. He felt adrift in limbo—and not a little scared. Judging by the worry lines on her forehead, Chlothilde felt the same. Like him, she didn't appear to be in the mood to spend time together. Henri called and let him know that the funeral would be on Tuesday, four days before the fight. Mobutu was laying it on thick: a full state funeral for Etienne. Martin was intrigued to see who would make an appearance. The major's service, on the other hand, was slated to be small, private, and discreet.

No surprise there. Martin figured he would attend Etienne's funeral with Henri and Chlothilde. One annoying piece of the puzzle remained impossible to place. Clearly, Russell had known he and Chlothilde would be vacationing at the family lodge—he had said as much shortly after Martin had picked up Chlothilde's note at the concierge desk at the hotel. How? The bastard always seemed to be one step ahead of everyone. Did he have a mole in Etienne's operation? For now, Martin had no choice but to let it ride. How he wished he could noodle through things with the major.

CHAPTER

24

THE FUNERAL WAS packed. Obviously, Mobutu had gone over-board to sell the cover story. There were more floral arrangements than Martin could count. The official army band, dressed in full uniform, played somber pieces for the occasion. The seating was formally arranged in order of importance, with ushers doing the seating. Martin and Chlothilde were in the third row with Henri. Martin had to resist the urge to laugh; only Chlothilde would have gotten the joke.

Mobutu showed up and gave a touching remembrance. Etienne's widow was either a great actress, or no one had told her the truth.

Martin glanced around and couldn't believe what he saw: Russell sitting prominently next to the aisle where he couldn't be missed.

Martin made eye contact. He had no choice. Mobutu must have been pissed, but there was little he could do without the proverbial smoking gun. After the service wound down, Mobutu made a point to slow down as he passed Russell's pew and nodded imperceptibly at him.

Touche, Martin thought, wondering if the menace he sensed in the gesture resonated at all with Russell. It was an

"I-know-where-you-live" moment. Martin knew who he would pick in that fight. Russell was a piranha to Mobutu's shark. They waited their turn and filed out into the bright sunlight.

True to form, Russell made a beeline toward Martin. "Terrible thing. I heard you almost got shot too. Who'd have thunk they were after Etienne, though he was kind of involved with the Mozambican government in trying to put down Frelimo."

Jesus, Martin thought, the fucker could lie with the best of them. That shouldn't have surprised him, but somehow the setting seemed to enhance the sin. "You sure it was Etienne they were after?"

"That's what a little birdie told me. Too bad the hit guys got done before they could be interrogated. I must go over and offer my condolences to Etienne's widow." The man could really lay it on thick.

Martin and Chlothilde stayed for a polite amount of time.

Chlothilde shivered as they got in the car. "That man scares me."

"He scares anyone with any sense."

Marten and Chlothilde headed back to her place. Martin should have been surprised to see Hippolyte waiting outside—a touch of normalcy is an otherwise surreal pastiche. He kissed Chlothilde and got in the car. No words were called for. They both knew what the deal was.

Hippolyte didn't need to say anything but kept glancing in the rearview mirror. Martin felt the tension. He wondered what kind of safehouse the major and Etienne had conjured up. He was sure that they had plenty to pick from. The obvious question was how safe would they really be. He felt the adrenalin rising in his gut and forced himself to keep looking at the side-view mirror.

Hippolyte was on the same page and obviously well trained. He smoothly executed a series of slick evasive maneuvers without changing expression.

Martin kept looking to make sure they weren't being tailed. It wasn't the time for half measures. "*Ca va*, Hippolyte?"

"Bien sur, mon ami."

A few minutes later, they pulled up in front of a travel agency in a commercial area of town that was popular with tourists. Perfect, Martin thought to himself. White folks going in and out wouldn't attract undue scrutiny. Someone knew what they were doing. He stepped inside, and the clerk didn't even look up from the ticket she was writing before waving him toward the back.

He went through the door to the back and found two obvious guard types standing in the hall in front of a door. They frisked him expertly, knocked, and waved him through. The major and Etienne were hunched over a map on a big table. They were both armed.

"I must say, Etienne, there was quite the turnout at your funeral. The president had very nice things to say about you."

"I am sure everyone was suitably impressed."

"Especially our good friend Russell. He made a point of going over to your wife."

Etienne grimaced. "It is hard to overstate his arrogance."

"Quite, and we shall make good use of it going forward." The major waved Martin to a chair by the table. "Just looking at things and getting our plans in order. As you know, we'll be headed out of town well before you, so we need to have our ducks in the same row."

Etienne rose. "I will leave you two to it. Monsieur le President has summoned me. "

The major walked Etienne to the door, ushered him past the guards, and then returned. "In case you hadn't tumbled it, we have a problem. Someone is leaking our plans. I'd hate to think it's Etienne, but there's no way Russell could have known where we were a few days back."

"They shot at him too."

"But did they, old boy? Easy enough to miss. I'm not certain. They could have been after both of us, granted, but how did they know we'd be there?"

"Tailed you?"

"Not possible. I've forgotten more about surveillance than this lot will ever know. We were clean."

"I assume you have thoughts."

"Only one thing to do play it straight and keep our eyes open. I suspect that the next time they try anything will be up country at the exchange."

"Things will be interesting with you and Etienne so close."

The major grimaced. "Best way, old man. Enemies closer and all that."

"So what's the plan going forward?"

"Steady as she goes for you. Just keep doing what you're supposed to be doing. I've changed up things a bit."

"Do tell."

"Well, for starters, I have a few arrangements to make on my own regarding our little insurance policy on Agent Russell."

"But Etienne knows about that."

"Of course, but there's that little bit of awkwardness, as we are both dead. He can't very well saunter into headquarters and set up a snatch on a US consular employee, can he?"

"Can you? You're also dead?"

"Quite, old boy, but I'm off the books on this one and not without resources."

"Someone told me once, always have them. Never let anyone know you have them."

"Whoever told you that was a wise man."

Martin wasn't sure, but the major almost looked like he was preening. "So I make like fight tourist for the next few days and await details."

"That's the deal. All a bit tedious. Waiting for the balloon to drop always is. However, I'm sure that Chlothilde will keep you from being entirely bored. You have to be disciplined, old cock. Life as normal."

"You're leaving soon. How will we stay in touch?"

"Can't use anyone we've used up to now, can we? I have some other resources. You'll know them when they say I come from Umbarara with a message."

"Sounds suitably melodramatic and easy to remember."

"Thought so. This is where the rubber meets the road. Tradecraft is important, especially now in the home stretch. We're playing for big stakes here with some seriously bad folks."

"I definitely get that."

"I would hope so after Lamu. So off with you now. Stay on your toes." The major patted him on the shoulder, which was about as close to showing affection as he got.

•••

Martin's thoughts were jumbled on the way back to Chlothilde's. He felt suddenly abandoned. His safety blankets—the major and Etienne—were gone. He realized that he hadn't felt this alone for a long time.

Chlothilde appeared to sense his mood as soon as he walked in. "You look strange. What happened?"

"Nothing in particular, and everything in general. You know the major is gone, so we're pretty much on our own."

"Maybe father could get some help."

"But who to trust after Etienne? I don't want to endanger either you or your family."

"Yes, that is difficult, but we must discuss this with Papa."

"Of course. Perhaps tonight at dinner. He'll be here soon."

• • •

The doorbell rang five minutes later. Henri gave Chlothilde a hug and took a seat. "*Eh bien, mes enfants*, where do we find ourselves? I can't believe that cretin Russell came to the funeral. Monsieur le President was seething."

"Somehow, I wasn't surprised," Martin said. "It was totally in character."

Henri nodded. "However, we have more serious concerns."

"Such as?"

"Where does Etienne fit in all of this?"

"That's exactly what concerns the major and I. The only one we figure that could have tipped Russell and his Cubans as to our whereabouts for the hit was Etienne."

"Mais non," Henri said with a furrowed brow, "but the Cubans tried to kill all of you."

"Or did they? We think they were only after the major. The rest was a show. We'll never know because the president showed up. But something's rotten in Kinshasa."

"Have you shared these thoughts with Monsieur le President?"

"Nope. Your job. I saw the major and Etienne briefly today. Right after Etienne took off for parts unknown, the major pulled me aside and shared his suspicions."

Henri's eyes widened in alarm. "Then we must terminate the operation immediately."

"That's exactly what we *can't* do. If we do, we'll never know who the real problem is here. Plus, we won't bag Tinner, Russell, the whole bent lot. It's in everyone's interest to clean it all up in one go."

"Yes, you are right," Henri said in a reluctant tone, "but it's a dangerous game."

"Agreed, but one we've already started. There's no backing out now if we want a good and final outcome. If we move prematurely, we'll never know who the traitor is. Plus, the president won't get his leverage for the big play. Speaking of which, where is he with all of this?"

Henri walked over to the bar and poured himself a scotch. "You all?"

"Not now. He must be scrambling. Etienne was his blue-eyed boy."

"I am sure. I will know soon enough. I have been summoned to a meeting with him shortly." Henri drained his scotch. "It is obvious that I must be the conduit between us as our friend Agent Russell will be watching like a hawk. There are only a few days to go."

"Okay, well, there's one nuance we discussed that you don't know about, and I think it's important."

Henri raised an eyebrow. "Eh bien?"

"We discussed grabbing Russell's girlfriend the night of the highjack as insurance against what are sure to be difficulties."

"I do like complete double-crosses."

"The issue is Etienne was party to that. If he's—"

"Yes, I see. I am sure Monsieur le President can think of something. I don't suppose we have any idea where Etienne has gone?"

Martin laughed. "He must have dozens of official and unofficial bolt holes."

Henri rose and headed for the door. "Sadly, you are no doubt right about that. Alors, mes enfants, I will come back after the meeting, and we can discuss everything over dinner."

CHAPTER

25

T**IME DRAGGED, BUT** Martin felt like he was in a time warp. He plopped down in a chair next to Chlothilde, who was already seated, and stared at the ceiling. "Weird. I feel like we're in suspended animation. I feel like there are things we should be doing, but they're not coming to me right now."

Chlothilde stretched and sighed. "I feel the same. I guess we will know more when Papa returns. I am scared. We really don't know whether Etienne is with Russell. I would never have believed he would betray the president."

"It's a hard one, but the major clearly suspects him, so that's enough for me. I don't see how we can do anything but assume the worst and hope to be surprised."

Chlothilde rose and took his hand. "Let's not just sit here. While we wait, how about a swim to clear our heads? By then, Papa will be back and we can at least have some concrete idea of where we are."

They swam and napped in the afternoon sun.

• • •

The faint sound of the doorbell roused Martin from a fitful sleep. He was still orienting himself when Henri strolled out on to the lanai.

"I am glad someone has been enjoying themselves and resting."

Chlothilde sat upright in her chaise lounge. "Touche, Papa. Was it interesting with Monsieur le President?"

"Interesting? I don't think so. Not the term I would use. He is extremely unhappy with many things and people. Luckily, we are not in that number or company."

"Etienne must give him pause."

"Bien sur, I know him very well, and I have only seen him this mad a few times. He kept asking, 'Who do I trust now?' All things considered, a very good question."

"And an obvious question," Martin said, "which none of us can answer. That said, I'm pretty sure I know what the major would say. Stick to the plan, double our watchfulness, and see what develops. It's not great, but I don't see any other choice."

"Exactly what the president said. We have to let Agent Russell hang himself. Otherwise, it's our word against his. Plus, if we snatch Tinner, the Amis will owe us big time. Lastly, we have to confirm who the traitor is."

Chlothilde stood up. "But that is so dangerous, Papa. We have no idea who to trust."

Henri hugged her. "But we do know who *not* to trust. That's an important start. The president is determined to let things run their course. There is no other way to determine who the traitors are in our midst and catch Agent Russell in the act."

"Why can't we just grab him now and make him talk?"

"The Amis would know immediately, and he could deny everything. We need the smoking gun and, just as importantly, the traitor it points to."

"Any specific instructions from the president?"

"Mais non, he doesn't want to do anything to arouse suspicions, but he is considering the possibility of doing something as a means of leveraging Russell. That would have to happen at the last minute and would of course be confidential until it happens."

Martin didn't bother to hide the frustration in his voice. "So the next three days I play Joe Boring?"

"Yes, I suggest you, with a little help from Chlothilde, play the pre-fight tourists. There certainly is enough hoopla and nonsense to keep one occupied."

· · ·

That didn't prove to be a hard assignment. Whether or not Mobutu had declared a national holiday, everyone except the hustlers making money one way or another off the fight seemed to be taking the week off. There was an undercurrent of excitement in the air, a visceral buzz. Not that Martin needed one. That copperish taste of adrenalin was a constant. There was plenty of distraction over the next two days, but it was hard for him to focus. He felt even more naked as the day approached without any safety blanket.

Two days before the big event, Hippolyte picked up Martin to go out to Chlothilde's but changed routes.

"What's up, Hippolyte? This isn't the normal route."

"Be patient and watch the mirror. We have to be sure that your Amis friend is not watching."

"That's suitably mysterious." Martin was tempted to ask if that applied to Etienne too but stifled the temptation. He assumed that Hippolyte reported to Etienne, but it was impossible to tell the players without a scorecard these days. Come to think of it, just about everyone in the equation was reporting to at least two masters. The only question was who was the real one.

After a seemingly random twenty minutes of evasive maneuvers, they pulled up to a private walled compound and drove through the gates. The place was jumping with security.

A pair of guards expertly frisked Martin before ushering him inside, where he found Henri and Mobutu waiting.

Mobutu waved him to a seat on the couch. "It is perhaps a little late, my friend, but it is time we held a serious chat. Especially since our trusted mutual friend is elsewhere."

"I agree, Monsieur le President, but I'm sure he's thinking a few steps ahead of all of us as usual. To me, the Etienne issue is key, but if I know the major, he's assuming Etienne is the problem and has a plan."

"Indeed, we can contain him now. However, I am less sure about Agent Russell. He is—we both know—dangerous and at this point pretty desperate. I think we must get some leverage."

"Well, Monsieur le President, we know where that is."

"Yes, we are watching her, but the timing must be just right. We can't be premature and alert Agent Russell. Also, there is the Etienne issue."

Martin nodded. "As for the timing, during the hijack, of course. As for Etienne, if he's the rat, Russell will be at ease, and she will be acting normal."

"Of course, but that does bring up one issue we have to discuss: communications."

"As in, Monsieur le President, there won't be any for key periods."

Mobutu cracked his knuckles and thought for a second. "Not in the traditional sense. While we may not be able to communicate, we will definitely be able to observe."

"Counting on that, because I'll be sitting out at the airstrip with no real idea what's happening unless you all can talk to the pilot, which I assume you will be."

"Of course, I have detailed my most trusted men for the job." Mobutu rose and shook his and Henri's hands. "Bonne chance to us all. This operation will be tricky but worth an immense amount to all of us, you included, if we pull it off."

Mobutu and his guards departed, leaving Martin with some troubling thoughts. What if the president's most trusted men were as bent as Etienne? What if it had been them all along and not Etienne?

Henri grimaced as he rose and headed for the door. "I think I know what you are thinking, and they are not good thoughts."

"It doesn't take a genius to know, just a paranoid to go there. Still, we're in for the proverbial pound now. Just hoping it's not of our flesh."

They parted in separate directions.

Martin tried to calm his nerves during the ride back to Chlothilde's. Thirty-six hours to go, and he had more questions than ever. He caught Hippolyte glancing at him a few times. "Do I look like a dead man walking?"

"Mais non, just so much has happened in such a short time, mon ami."

"You got that right, and I don't know which end is up, so I'm going to keep moving and await developments. Just hoping I'm on the side of the good guys."

"You are. I heard the president say so before I left to get you. He trusts the major completely, which means he trusts you."

"Well, that's something, but I have the sinking feeling that more, much more, will somehow be required."

The rest of the ride passed in a nervous silence.

• • •

The evening with Chlothilde proved to be a struggle for Martin, and he sensed she, too, was grappling with anxiety. Conversation was difficult. Until the operation was over, nothing would be remotely normal. They made love with intense passion but had nothing to say afterward.

THE HOTEL WAS fast approaching madhouse status as Martin picked his way through the lobby to the restaurant the next morning. It was a colorful crowd, multi-hued, polyglot. This truly was the first global boxing event, and as far as he could recollect, the first non-Olympic event financed by a government. Somehow, the audacity of it seemed to make a perfect backdrop for what was going to be an equally historic crime.

His generous tipping had paid off. His normal table was available—but not empty.

"You're looking awfully pensive."

Fuck, he hated how Russell could materialize out of nowhere.

"How about you buy me a coffee while we review plans?"

It wasn't a question. "I certainly hope everything's locked in on your side. It is on mine."

"Yep, my guys are all set."

He must have an inexhaustible supply, Martin thought to himself. There wasn't the slightest hint in Russell's mannerisms or voice that anything outside of the original plan had happened.

Martin kept his face blank. The difference was he had to really think about it and concentrate. "All good. I'll be out at the strip from six p.m. tomorrow night. Don't expect to see you all until sometime after ten, though."

Russell's intense stare was discomfiting.

Martin forced himself to stay focused. "You and how many others will be making the flight? The Antonov is big, but the weight will affect fuel consumption."

"Don't worry about that. We've done our sums. Everything will be fine. You just have that bird ready to fly."

"Of course, and you remember that that letter is sitting out there if you pull anything. When I get back here safe, it will be destroyed as soon as the money hits my account."

"That will be a good day for both of us."

Russell stood. "See you tomorrow night. I don't have to say the obvious."

No, he didn't. Martin felt his stomach tighten. Game time was coming, and all he wanted was for it to start.

• • •

Martin had dinner with Chlothilde, but it was an exercise in awkwardness. They toyed with their food and gave up on idle conversation after a few minutes. He had only one thing on his mind, and it was obvious she was similarly preoccupied. Discussing it would have yielded nothing but increased anxiety. They embraced fiercely.

"I'm planning on being back in three days," he said. "Let's go somewhere nice and celebrate."

"Sounds lovely. I will research and plan it while you are away. I know Papa will be with the president monitoring things."

"I'm sure they'll be following closely, but you're not likely to know much until it's over and mission accomplished."

• • •

Back at the hotel, he tossed and turned restlessly. It wasn't like he really expected to sleep, but he couldn't force himself to think about anything but the next day and night. Bad, slow-motion playbacks of the night at the beach in Lamu kept repeating themselves. Everything was the familiar monochrome, fade-to-black nightmare, except for one glaring change. Instead of Esther, it was Chlothilde. He kept trying to erase the image, but it kept replaying until he lapsed into a trance-like state between sleep and reality.

He awoke the next morning in the usual state: covered in sweat, tangled in sheets. Finally, the day was at hand. He showered and headed down to breakfast, not that he was in the slightest bit hungry. The hotel lobby and dining room were a seething mass of fight people. The buzz was visceral but lost in the shuffle as far as he was concerned.

He forced down the eggs, not tasting them but knowing he'd need fuel for later. The action in the lobby was colorful, to say the least. Many of the punters were getting started early. Martin was momentarily bummed by the fact that he wouldn't see the fight. Eyes on the prize, he reminded himself. That was what highlight reels were for.

He had debated checking out but decided against it, partly out of superstition, partly out of pragmatism. He went up to his room and got organized—not that he was going to be taking anything. Hippolyte was due midafternoon. Martin sat on the balcony and watched the street below. It wasn't hard to tell something major was up. Hawkers and hustlers were milling about—piranhas closing in on the kill. A few policemen half-heartedly tried to shoo them away, but it was useless.

Martin waited to go downstairs until he saw Hippolyte pull up and station himself a block down from the entrance. It was still a struggle to get to the car.

"*Mon Dieu, C'est fou*," Hippolyte said somewhat needlessly.

"You're right. It's a good thing we're going the opposite direction."

Once they cleared the neighborhood, things settled down. They were headed away from 20 May Stadium, the site of the fight.

"Monsieur Martin, I have a message. I was told to tell you that the matter you were concerned about has been dealt with."

"Okay, that's good news."

Martin mostly tuned out on the long drive out to Matete. Funny, but now that things were getting real, he felt strangely detached, like he was outside of himself observing his own reactions. *Better enjoy numb while it lasts*, he thought ruefully. *Things are about to get really interesting.*

They pulled into the strip at Matete about thirty minutes later.

Lucienne was tinkering with one of the engines. "Just running through the final checks."

"I should hope so. Obviously, we can't afford any problems tonight." Martin handed him a fat envelope.

"Don't worry, I have triple-checked everything. All good. I have something for you." Lucienne handed him a pistol. "It's a Smith and Wesson. The major personally selected it for you. He said you were familiar with it. Here's two extra clips. He said to tell you—"

"That if I need more, we're buggered," Martin said, finishing Lucienne's sentence.

Another one of the major's life lessons, usually delivered with the unapologetic coda, "If you only ever use it once, it will be worth all the times you listened to it."

Martin inserted a clip, racked it, and flicked the safety on. He caught Lucienne's glance. "I assume you'll be carrying also."

"Bien sure, but I think we cannot be obviously armed when our friend Mr. Russell pulls up."

"For sure. I assume you have some good places to hide them. Can't be any shortage in the Antonov."

"Yes, but hiding them and being able to access them easily if something goes wrong are not necessarily the same thing."

"You got that right, but you've been at this a while. Show me."

The interior of the Antonov was furnace-hot. The heat mixed with the overpowering fumes of aviation fuel and lubricating oil made Martin momentarily dizzy.

Lucienne led him along the fuselage to where a large first aid box was attached to the fuselage. He slid out one side, revealing a holster attached to the fuselage. He signaled Martin to hand him the pistol, which fit perfectly into the holster.

"Nice. How many other hidey-hides do you have?"

"This is the only one back here. The one in the cockpit will do you little good, for you will never be flying this thing."

"True, but you never know."

Lucienne led him up to the cockpit. He showed martin a similarly positioned holster under the seat.

Martin noticed all the instruments were still labeled in Cyrillic. "You speak Russian?"

"No, I know them by heart. I have been flying this bird for five years. She has never let me down."

Martin tried unsuccessfully to nap during the rest of the afternoon.

• • •

It was a relief when the sun set, but Martin's tension level ratcheted up. "I wish we weren't operating under radio silence."

"Yes, it is awkward but necessary. I doubt we will see or hear anything before midnight."

"Yep, the problem for me is that we have two sets of uncertainty: what's happening here and what's happening up north."

"There is too much to think about. Let's try to eat. I have some sandwiches and some water. Who knows when we will get the chance to eat again."

The cheese sandwich was tasteless, but Martin forced it down. He also forced himself to drink the whole liter bottle of water. They were going from humid forest to dry desert. Either way, he'd need hydration. He tried not to check his watch too often.

At last, two vehicles approached slowly, their headlights temporarily blinding him. The first stopped just short of Martin.

Russell climbed out and gave Martin a mock salute. "I brought you a nice surprise. You're going to love it." He circled to the rear door and dragged back a hooded, handcuffed person beside him. "Rise and shine, Ms. Chlothilde. Your lover boy is here. Unfortunately, he can't do much to help you except be on his best behavior."

Chlothilde sobbed. "Oh, Martin, I am so sorry. He came with three men. They shot the guard Papa posted."

Russell herded her toward the plane. "Just be an obedient little girl, and everything will be fine." He glowered at Martin. "You too, Fine. No BS, or she goes right before you do." He signaled the other vehicle to pull forward.

Two Cubans jumped out and began loading heavy crates into the plane. When they were done, they thoroughly searched Martin and Lucienne. After Russell waved them off, they wordlessly jumped into the vehicle and left.

"Well, that leaves just the three of us. One happy family."

Martin was grimly digesting the implications of Russell's coup de main. One possibility was he was going to just make them disappear and bluff his way through things on his return to Kinshasa. Martin discarded that theory as quickly as he thought it. It clearly wouldn't work. No, there was only one option: he was going to do the deal and keep going to his new best friend in Tripoli. Not good news. He wasn't a loose-ends type of guy.

"Let's saddle 'em up." Russell punctuated the command by none too gently shoving Chlothilde toward the stairs. "I'm sure they're anxiously awaiting us up north."

Martin followed them up the stairs. Lucienne brought up the rear and latched the door behind them.

Russell unlocked the cuffs on Chlothilde and pushed her down on one of the benches that lined the fuselage. "You." He gestured at Martin with the pistol. "Up to the cockpit with your buddy. I want you all in front of me. No more surprises this evening."

Martin blew Chlothilde a kiss and followed Lucienne forward. *There'd better be some more surprises*, he thought to himself. Truth be told, he had absolutely no idea what was going to be waiting for him, and that scared the shit out of him.

Lucienne handed him a set of headphones and started running through his preflight ritual.

Martin heard a click in his headphones.

"Well, Mr. Fine, your Amis friend has made his first mistake: not taking away our ability to talk to each other."

"That's true, and the fact that he's not worried about radioing ahead tells me he's very confident of the facts on the ground up north."

"True, but he also is holding a gun on Chlothilde. What are you going to do about that?"

"That hasn't escaped my attention—or the fact that there isn't much I can do about it right now."

Lucienne finished his check and fired the engines, which caught with a few staccato bangs before settling into a throaty roar. They taxied out to the dimly lit strip. Lucienne didn't seem fazed by the lack of light. No surprise. Martin figured he had probably done this in his sleep countless times. It was a long, slow climb to cruising altitude, but Lucienne kept it below oxygen-mask level.

The plane leveled off, and Lucienne flicked some switches and took his hands off the yoke. "Autopilot for the next few hours, my friend."

"Not that I plan on relaxing. I wish we were fucking there."

"I understand. I have done this hundreds of times. It never gets easier."

Martin looked back through the open door to the cockpit.

Chlothilde gave him a weak smile. Russell put his hand on his pistol and gave him a thumbs-up.

Martin glanced at Lucienne, and the intercom clicked.

"He's a bad one, and I've known more than a few in my lifetime. I hope your friend the major is up to the task."

"When it comes to devious, he wrote the book. I'm counting on him being ahead of whatever's developed. He always lectures me about fourth-circle thinking."

"What's that?"

"It comes from the rock-in-the-pond metaphor. Most people only think one or two ripples out from the point of impact. The major likes to think four or five out. I guess it's a kind of three-dimensional chess exercise. He always told me that most Westerners are one- or two-circle types. The Russians play the long game. Hence their affinity for chess."

"I am getting a headache thinking about it. I'd rather just fly."

And fly they did through the dark tropical night. Normally, the African night this close to the equator was luminous with the stars so bright they seemed to pulse in the sky. Not tonight. The darkness was squid-ink black. Not for the first time Martin understood the aptness of Conrad. They were truly flying blind into the proverbial heart of darkness. The last time he'd done that, he'd ended up emotionally scalded. He suddenly felt ice cold. He shivered and shook himself like a dog.

"What's up, friend? You look troubled."

"Just hoping not to repeat history." Martin was glad Lucienne didn't follow up. He wouldn't have answered anyway. He focused on the instruments and forced himself to think about what was awaiting them.

Sometimes, he glanced back, hoping Russell might be sleeping or at least nodding off. No chance. He saw from Chlothilde's body language that she was terrified.

He clicked the intercom. "How much longer?"

"At least ninety minutes."

Scary as things were going to get, the wait was going to be worse. He closed his eyes and tried to blank out.

The next thing he knew, Lucienne was elbowing him. "Thirty minutes out."

Russell must have sensed something from the change in the timber of the engines. He handcuffed Chlothilde to the bench and made his way forward. "Looks like we're almost there. I'll just plunk myself down in the jump seat. I don't have to say the obvious." He gestured back toward Chlothilde with his pistol.

Martin had been waiting for this moment. "Well, Russell, we have a little surprise for you too. Guess who's waiting for us when we land: a certain little lady that you're rather fond of. The major's profound distrust of you seems to have been very well-placed."

"The old fox. I should have known. Things are going to get interesting in a little while."

Martin wouldn't have wanted to play poker with Russell. He was almost as inscrutable as the major. But not quite. And nowhere near as smart, which Martin was counting on.

They droned on into the night.

A few minutes later, Martin spotted a series of lights up ahead as they rapidly lost altitude. Squinting, he was able to make out a line of trucks framing a crude runway.

Lucienne keyed his mic. "How come you tipped our hand?"

"To make sure Russell didn't just shoot us when we landed and let his cronies take care of everyone else on our team on the ground. You land here before?"

"A couple of times, but not with this kind of reception committee."

Lucienne landed smoothly enough and taxied toward the trucks. As he was slowing the plane to a halt, Russell headed back to the cabin. As soon as he turned his back, Lucienne pulled his pistol from under the seat and handed it to Martin, who quickly concealed it under his shirt.

Russell pulled Chlothilde to her feet and signaled for her and Martin to deplane in front of him.

The glare of the headlights blinded Martin as they climbed down the steps. So much for getting the drop on Russell. Anyway, Martin had dismissed the thought as soon as it entered his mind. He still didn't have a clue who was actually in charge at the bottom of the steps.

Martin felt a surge of relief when the major stepped forward.

"Martin, glad to see you. I assume Chlothilde is a surprise from our friend Agent Russell. What a disappointment it's going to be for him when he sees our little surprise."

"I told him about it. Didn't want him to shoot us out of hand as we got out while his buddies did you all."

The major seemed unperturbed. "Well, Agent Russell, it's really good to see you, especially under these circumstances. I don't know who's going to savor this moment more: Mr. Fine or myself. Of course, there's also Mobutu, who I think is preparing a rather special reception for you when we get back to Kinshasa."

Etienne stepped forward, revealing himself. "*Desole* for all of you, but some of us, including Monsieur Russell, have quite different plans for the rest of the evening." He motioned three soldiers with AKs forward.

The soldiers expertly frisked the major and Martin, disarming them.

Chlothilde sobbed. "You too, Etienne? I cannot believe it."

"I am actually sorry you had to be involved, Chlothilde. I am very fond of you and your father, but Monsieur Russell has made me an offer I can't refuse."

The soldiers—Cubans, Martin noticed—herded Chlothilde, the major, and him to the side. Where had they all come from?

Etienne waved forward a white man in rumpled khakis. "Bien. *Monsieur le Docteur*, check the material."

Tinner climbed up into the plane. The major appeared to be studying his surroundings, but the Cubans weren't paying much attention. Afterall, there wasn't anywhere to go or any way to outrun an AK round.

"Well, wish I could say I was surprised," the major whispered to Martin.

"I'm assuming by that statement that you have something up your sleeve."

"Of course, old boy. I have a Plan C. That's the good news. The bad news is that we have to figure out a way to survive or convince them not to kill us before they leave."

"And?"

"At this stage, they really have no need to. Mobutu knows everything. Etienne will have told Agent Russell that, and he's too much of a pro to make unnecessary enemies of my lot. Nope. He'll leave us to report back to an extremely pissed off Mobutu."

"Hope you're right like you usually are."

They didn't have to wait long to find out. Dr. Tinner and

Russell emerged from the plane, and Etienne ordered the Cubans to load the crates in the truck.

Russell sauntered over, smugness oozing out of every pore. "Well now, Major, I've been thinking exactly what to do with you all. I could, of course, shoot you out of hand, but I don't think it would be half as satisfying as leaving you to go back with your tail between your legs and report your abject failure to President Mobutu, who will not have kind words for your superiors in London."

"Damm you, Russell. What an ignominious end to my career: to be outwitted by you of all people."

"Glad to oblige, Major. In the meantime, I do need a little collateral in case you have any more tricks up your sleeve. I think Chlothilde will do nicely." He grabbed Chlothilde and started shoving her toward the truck. He motioned his girlfriend toward the truck. "You too, darling. So nice of the major to think of bringing you along."

"But I don't want to live in Libya."

Without hesitating, Russell shot her in the head.

Martin and the major moved forward but stopped when Russell put a round in the sand near their feet.

"I wouldn't if I were you. The only person in this whole mess I care less about than her is the lovely Chlothilde." With that, Russell signaled the Cubans to cover them as he and Etienne dragged Chlothilde toward the truck.

After everyone was loaded, Russell flipped them a mock salute. "Be glad I'm feeling I owe you after Lamu, or you'd be as dead as she is. I can't say it's been nice, but it's been real."

The truck roared off into the darkness, leaving them momentarily paralyzed.

Martin tried to suppress the urge to panic. "Okay, Major, you're the man with all the answers. What do we do now?"

"Well, old cock, we execute Plan D." He gestured to Lucienne. "Please find something to cover her with. I don't feel good about her, but who would have thought he would be such a bastard? That's one mistake I will take to the grave with me."

"Yeah, not quite Lamu, but close. I knew he was a bastard." Martin shook his head in disgust. "Okay, so what now? I am all ears for Plan D."

"Right. Coming right up, but first, let's get into the plane. Then I will need the radio." He turned to Lucienne. "Warm up the engines while you're at it. Plan D coming up."

Once inside the cockpit, the major fiddled with the radio, trying several frequencies until he got the one he wanted.

Lucienne looked at him enquiringly. "Where are we going?"

"About fifty miles north heading two-seventy." The major clicked the handset twice. "Mamba One, Mamba One, come in."

"Mamba One here, Major. We have them surrounded. Are you en route?"

"Yes, no more than twenty minutes."

"Okay, we are commencing the ambush."

"Be careful of the woman if you can. She's important to us."

"Who's that?" Martin asked as he retrieved his pistol from behind the emergency medical kit and racked it.

"Hasan Habre, useful chap, commandant of a group called Frolinat. They're trying to take over Chad. You know how quickly things change around here. Two weeks ago, Gaddafi and Tombalbaye were at loggerheads, but Gaddafi decided he didn't want Frolinat on his border. He called up Tombalbaye and said he was no longer supporting Frolinat."

"And the rest is history. Okay, how'd you know?"

The major gave him a pained look. "Friends in low places."

"Question withdrawn."

They landed at another crude strip about twenty minutes later.

There were several jeeps waiting.

A camouflage-clad soldier stepped forward and snapped off a salute. "Commandant Habré at your service. I've been looking forward to meeting you, Major. President Mobutu has told me much about you."

The major offered a tight-lipped smile. "Likewise. Pleasure to meet you. But no time for pleasantries now."

Habré waved them into a jeep. "Allez-y! They're about five miles away."

They sped off into the darkness. Martin couldn't see much, and he was petrified for Chlothilde.

They screeched to a halt a few minutes later and immediately heard a fierce firefight.

As tracers zipped into the night sky, Habré motioned them to get out of the jeep and take cover.

Another soldier slithered out of the darkness and reported to Habré.

"Okay, mes Amis. My men have captured the two trucks with the Uranium. That's the good news. The bad is that the third truck with Russell, the other Blanc, and the hostage is surrounded, but they haven't surrendered. They want to parlay." Habré motioned them into the jeep, "We will proceed very slowly."

The truck was stopped about five hundred yards from the border post. Habré's men were fanned out around it in a circle. Searchlights from the guard towers swept back and forth across the frozen tableau.

Martin fought off another wave of fear. "Fuck, Major, I don't suppose you have a Plan E sitting around, do you?"

"Actually, old man, it's plan I for *improvise*. Let's see what Mr. Russell has to say for himself. He's got Chlothilde but not much else at this point. He's burned his bridges. The proof of that is lying in the plane."

Habré signaled the jeep forward slowly. He and the major followed carefully, using it as cover. They stopped about fifty feet short of the surrounded truck.

"Well, well, Agent Russell," the major said, "things can certainly change fast around here. Hard to keep track. Are we on the third or fourth cross? Anyway, much as it pains me, I'm prepared to allow you, Tinner, and Etienne to cross over the border and take your chances with the mad colonel. Bad as that alternative might be, I can assure you he'll treat you better than Mobutu."

"It pains me to admit, Major, but that is acceptable to me."

"Okay, so tell your buddies at the border crossing to douse the lights. Then you are all going to get out of the truck slowly and start to walk backward toward the border crossing. You've got at least ten Ak-47s on you, so no funny business."

Habré and three soldiers stepped into the light halo from the truck's headlights and trained their weapons on Russell, Etienne, Tinner, and Chlothilde as they clambered down.

Martin started forward, trying to make eye contact with Chlothilde. Her eyes were wide with fear.

Time seemed to slow down as they backed up toward the border. There were three pistols trained on Chlothilde.

Suddenly, a shot cracked out, and Etienne crumpled to the sand. Martin dashed toward Chlothilde and tackled her, scrambling to cover her as he tried to pull out his pistol.

The night was illuminated by muzzle flashes from every direction. Martin felt a sharp pain in his shoulder and was shocked to see he'd been hit. He was strangely numb as he watched the blood run down his arm.

Habré's men were laying down withering fire. So were the Libyans. Several troops on each side crumpled to the sand, but miraculously, Tinner and Russell made it across the border unscathed.

Both sides ceased fire of their own accord. Habré's men covered Martin and Chlothilde as they crawled out of range.

"A nice souvenir for you, Martin. Painful no doubt, but it won't kill you." The major helped him to a jeep. "Chlothilde, are you okay?"

"Yes, it's a miracle. It's like a bad dream is ending. Martin, thank you. I'd like to hug you, but how can I without hurting you?"

Martin winced at every bounce of the jeep.

Once they got to the plane, the major retrieved the first aid kit and did some doctoring.

Martin was impressed. "Not bad, Major."

"Piece of cake. You're lucky. The bullet went right through. Didn't tear anything irreplaceable. Good tale for your grandchildren when you have them."

Habré joined them. "My men are refueling the plane, Major. Then we must depart."

"Good show, Hasan. I'm sure that the president will be even more generous now that we have the uranium back. Too bad we missed out on Russell and Tinner, but one can rarely have it all. Besides, getting Etienne out of the works is big."

Habré and his men finished refueling the plane just as a spectacular dawn illuminated the sky.

"There's something special about the desert light," the major said, "especially after a successful bit of drama."

Martin grit his teeth. "I don't like that Russell got away."

"Yes, unfortunate that, but this isn't Hollywood. We got the uranium back, the Mad Colonel was stymied, and the hero and heroine live to fight another day. Not Hollywood, but not all bad."

Martin hugged Chlothilde. "Definitely a better ending than Part One. Somehow, I think there may end up being a Part Three."

The major chuckled. "Quite possible, old cock."

JOHN KWELI is an old hand in Africa, having
endured sixteen coups, six civil wars, two
genocides, and many other things best forgotten.
His is a false name, but everything in this book
happened, as the guilty know.